This is a work of fiction. Names, characters, places, and incidents either are the product of the author's imagination or are used fictitiously. Any resemblance to actual events, locales, organizations, or persons, living or dead, is entirely coincidental and beyond the intent of either the author or the publisher.

Touching Evil
TOP SHELF
An imprint of Torquere Press Publishers
PO Box 2545
Round Rock, TX 78680
Copyright © 2006 by Rob Knight
Cover illustration by Plutocat
Published with permission
ISBN: 1-934166-03-0, 978-1-934166-03-1
www.torquerepress.com

First Torquere Press Printing: October 2006
Printed in the USA

Chapter One

It is simply a matter of patience, being a collector. He has to wait and watch for just the right thing to wander by – it can't be exactly like any of the others, but it needs to be in the same vein, have the same tones. The same flavors. He knows -- he knew when he saw his most current acquisition, he knew that was the next piece, the next bit of perfection.

The new ones were always the most perfect, the most pristine.

The surge of electricity when he sees them – through a window, in a store, in a library, in a grainy photo in the newspaper – it can make him weak in the knees, make his mouth water and his heart pound.

He turns the light on over the worktable, the single bulb swinging idly as he hand-primed the grinder, starting it moving. The little sparks as metal met belt reminded him of fireflies and picnics on the Fourth of July, sitting on the sand on Wrightsville beach and watching the lights in the sky, the answering lights in the glass jar he carried with him.

Firefarts, his father had called them, lighting another cigarette, eyes staring out over the ocean. Friggin' firefarts.

Nothing permanent. Just seconds of beauty. Like his collection – pure distant beauty, just for a moment, captured forever before they were ruined, spark gone.

His fireflies.

His to collect. To keep.

***

Dark. It was dark; how could it be dark already? Unreasonably dark, dark enough that it seemed to cling to his skin like oil.

Greg walked forward, bare feet splashing, landing on smooth, slick flooring. He took one reluctant step at a time, hands held in front of him, fingertips stretched back as if recoiling from what they were going to encounter. Nothing he would find here would be good. Nothing could be, covered with this slime of darkness.

He could hear things, muffled cries and mutters, soft words.

If he was a stronger man, he would turn, would turn around and run toward the door and the light and the...

Oh.

He fought the urge to cry out as his hands brushed a curtain, slick and warm like a shower curtain in a public bathroom, fingers curling into it even as his instinct was to pull away, let go. He wasn't a stronger man. He hadn't been able to fight this then; he couldn't now. He took a breath, breathed in the heaviness, the black, the ink of the air.

Then he wrenched open the curtain, eyes wide, and stepped into someone's nightmare.

Hours later, when the dawn was breaking, Greg Pearsall found himself crumpled on the floor of his bookstore, drenched in sweat even in the chill of a late October night, a book clenched in his hands like it was a life preserver. His cry startled him, surprised out of him by the pain of unclenching his hands. He wouldn't be able to move them tomorrow, the knuckles already red and swollen. It was no easy task – God knew he wasn't twenty anymore – but he unfolded himself, and found his glasses, before fumbling for the phone on the counter and dialing a number he knew better than his own. He waited until the machine picked up, listening to the laconic voice telling him to leave a message or hang the fuck up, then he left his message.

"It's me. It's happened again. You know where I am."

Or where he would be in an hour, after he stumbled upstairs to his loft, showered, and changed into something less... atrocious.

Greg left the book on the floor, among the wrapping and the rest of the mail that had fallen, and pulled out his elevator key, listening to the creak and rumble of the old girl. Alice would get whatever was still on the floor when she opened The Candle's End in a few hours, sorting the pamphlets into psychics wanting clients, the latest improvement in herbal supplements that increased libido – trash – and publishers' catalogs – his in-box – and the new tarot samples – display counter. He couldn't care less.

He wanted the man off his skin, out of his blood. He wanted heat and steam and…

Oh. Oh, thank God he had a sliding glass door on his shower.

Thank God.

He turned the stereo on, Arabic music filling the air and his head, pounding through the empty space, keeping him company as he let the water pour over him. Relax him. Ease him. Home. Safe. Home.

Safe.

Be at peace.

When he got out of the shower, though, he almost jumped out of his skin, tension slamming back into him in a rush. The only reason he didn't was because the brick shit house sitting on his toilet was one he knew. Artie. Detective Arthur McAdams.

Jesus fuck, the man was quiet.

"You made good time." He grabbed one of his towels and started drying off, sluicing the water off his own skinny-assed limbs. He knew he'd eventually regret giving Artie a key, but...

Hell, some things were necessary.

Artie was necessary.

The baseball cap came off, Artie running his rough fingers through that straw blond hair, too early to be in work mode, still blinking slow. "I came ASAP. No traffic. Wanted to make sure you were... Well. Last time I found you on the floor, man."

Artie's shirt was inside out and the short-cropped hair looked vaguely like the cat had been wallowing in it. Artie needed a hat in the worst way.

"I just got up off the floor. I need to start opening the mail on the sofa." He should have known when the package came in with the Candle's End mail, no return address, no nothing. After that fucking reporter wrote that article on him a year ago, there was no telling what came in. Christ, he was tired of old rings, old letters – "can you find this person," "what can you tell me about that?" Like he was a side-show freak, something from daytime TV.

"You all right?" He could feel those cool gray cop's eyes all over him, sizing him up.

"It wasn't pleasant. I left... the book and the packaging are downstairs. I won't touch it again. There's blood on the cover." He slipped into his sweats and sighed, drying off his hair. "He sent it to me, directly."

"So he knows who you are. What you do." Artie stood up and almost...almost reached for him. He could feel the warmth of that big hand hovering just below his elbow. "Let's go out and sit. Get you orange juice. Get my notebook."

Shit, he must be looking shocky. Artie wasn't giving him any hassle. He was feeling shocky, even after the shower, even now in his own little sanctuary. His hidey-hole. His neat, pristine, nicely decorated, feng shui-approved prison.

He nodded to Artie, letting the detective lead the way. Ten years. Ten years since the accident -- one misstep, one head meeting concrete stairs, and three days in a coma and nothing ever went back to normal. Not a thing.

Damn it.

"There's coffee. I started it before this all started . French roast. Good stuff."

"Heavy cream and sugar, then." Artie led the way out, waving him toward the couch. "I'll get it."

He nodded, sitting on his sofa, fingers sliding over the white corduroy and finding a blissful silence inside. This one had only ever been his, the cloth and wood telling him nothing at all. "I saw your partner on the television yesterday. Congratulations on your arrest."

"Thanks." Cups clinked together, the refrigerator door thumping open and closed as Artie moved around his kitchen like a man who belonged there. "It was good to wrap that one up."

"Leah looked tired. Tell her I have some of that tea she wanted. It came in with the last shipment of astralagus and that hideous diet tea that smells like old bed sheets." Honestly. Diet tea. Retail could be most foul. Of course, he could always close the Candle when something... untoward happened. It had been much harder to explain during his basic anatomy seminar lectures.

Panicky freshmen.

"I will." Artie came back and handed him the cup, Artie's fingers very carefully not touching his. "She likes that stuff. Not the diet. The other."

Greg nodded his thanks, drank deep, the coffee warming him inside, burning all the way down from his lips to his toes. God, he could sleep for a month.

Waiting until Greg'd drank halfway down, Artie sat back and got his notebook out, a steno deal, simple and plain. Kinda like Artie. The pen was nice though. He'd used it once. It had been a gift from Artie's sister, Agatha. Agatha used to think Artie was a pain, but she loved him dearly now, adored him. Thought he was the best brother ever...

Oh, fuck. Stop it. Stop. It.

He rubbed his forehead, thinking, trying to focus on the last thing on earth he wanted to focus on. Old book. Heavy. The blood stain looked like a flowering tree branch, just drooping... "The package was plain. The book was old. Hardback. From a library. There was blood on the cover."

They always started like this. Simple things. Normal things. Things anyone could see.

"Back up. Did you save the packaging?" Scribbling, Artie glanced up at him and back at the page, cagey. Judging his mood. He was getting used to the man knowing him almost better than he did, even if it chafed like hell.

"Yes. It's downstairs with the book. On the floor by my desk."

"Okay. I'll have a look. You know the drill." He did. They'd take it in for evidence, etc., etc. "What kind of book was it?"

"A medical text. Surgery. I didn't get to open it. The spine was broken, torn up." It had smelled bad when he'd torn the paper off -- rotten, spoiled. The words had been gold once, but they were still raised. Embossed.

"Fuck. Something you'd be interested in. This guy is scary." The pen scratched loudly for a minute, the only other sound the tiny noise of his fingers on the couch, rubbing. His home. His place.

Greg nodded, head feeling a little like a bobble-head doll, the memories starting to slide along his synapses. "She's young and somewhere very dark, underground maybe. Warm, even now. The only light is red. She was still alive when he sent the book. It's her blood on it, not his. It's his book. He loves his books. He sent it because she ruined it.

There was water. His knife is short, curved, like a claw."

He put the coffee cup down. He hated this part. Remembering this was like a dream, something that couldn't be real. Shouldn't be real.

"She. Okay, so he's got a girl. Young how? Baby? Kid? Teenager?"

Greg frowned, drawing his feet into Indian style, ankles dragging along the sofa fabric. Her. It was a her. A girl. Painted and primped and crying. "I... Not a baby. She's got makeup on, though."

"Yeah? Is she old enough to have boobs?" So delicate. Lord.

"It was dark. Maybe? She's not naked. He wasn't going to rape her. He wanted to cut her. Fix… fix her?" His fingers moved faster, pushing the memories away. Not in him. Not in his head.

Those eyes peered at him over the top of the notebook, Artie's blond brows drawing together. The chair creaked as Artie got up and came to squat in front of him, hand resting next to his right knee.

"'S'okay, man. We don't have to think about that right now. Just what I ask, remember? One little bit at a time."

"Right." He took a deep breath, looking right at Artie. Home. Safe. Sanctuary. The man knew how to help him, how this worked; he just had to trust in it. Trust Artie. This was old hat. "One detail at a time."

"Let's go around the girl right now and break it down. You said red light was the only light. What kind? Emergency tunnel lights? Stoplight lights? Construction lights?"

"They moved, swinging or blinking or something. Dull dark red. They went slow."

"'Kay. What about the water? Deep or shallow? What did it smell like?" Yeah. Yeah, he could do it this way.

He leaned back, eyes on the mural painted on the ceiling – blue and grays and white, all swirled and peaceful and... He could see hints and whispers, remember the way he'd stared and gagged. Remember the water on his bare feet. Between his toes. "It was enough to get your feet wet. Enough to splash. The place smelled dead, foul, like rotted flesh."

"Decomp, huh? Gross." His coffee cup got a push, right under his nose so all he could smell was java and cream, and the gag reflex he hadn't even noticed eased. "But it wasn't deep. Not like an underground feed?"

"I don't know. It was definitely under the ground, but it was a place, a man-made place, not a cave."

"The floor. Was it metal or stone?"

"Not metal. It didn't ring. It echoed. Concrete? The book didn't echo when he dropped it, just his footsteps." Her blood had dropped on the book, fat drops from her fingers. "She bit her nails."

"Then we ought to be able to get a good sample." Sometimes it made him crazy that Artie compartmentalized. Sometimes it helped. "What about the knife? You said it was custom?"

"I said it was little. Curved. Like a finger. Like his fingers, held against his hand." He held up one finger, curled it like a claw. A shiny, sharp claw. "He touches her with it."

"Close your eyes and tell me what it looks like. Silver? Black handle? Does it have any chasing on the blade?"

"The blade is silver, sharp, shiny shiny shiny. There's no handle, just a blade with a hole in the bottom." He could almost see the man. Almost. Weird, because he didn't. Not usually. Not usually, but he could almost see, even if it didn't work that way.

"The guy's a regular ball of fun. Okay. All right. Did you see anything else? Her clothes? His? His hand? What did it look like?"

He must be looking edgy. Artie was wrapping up. They'd do this again and again, he knew.

"Yeah. His fingers were crook..." He frowned, a flash from last night hitting him deep and low, bending him over his own hands. "Blonde. She was blonde, Artie. All of them have been and the next is going to be, too."

Artie caught his coffee cup as it fell. "Then we'll look for more. Try to find his pattern. That's enough for now."

The stubble covered the little scar right above Artie's upper lip. The scar Artie got when he fell off the jungle gym in Mrs. Marsh's fourth grade class and Janie Potts laughed at him and made him cry.

Greg nodded. Yes. Yes, okay. Enough. Enough. He'd washed, but he could feel the blood on his fingers, in the ridges of his fingerprints. "Why didn't he send the book to the police, the media?"

"Because they can't do what you do. You want some food?" Joints popped as Artie levered up. "You caught me just as I was about to share a TV dinner with Duke."

"Those things are atrocious and not for breakfast." He stood up, stretched as tall as he could go, the loft spinning around him. "I should have real food in there."

Grinning, Artie nodded. "And I can even cook it. What do you want, man?"

Yeah. It was good to have someone to pull him out of it. To make things normal.

"Grilled cheese and tomato soup." He winced, but refused to take it back. It was comfort food and it was going to comfort him. Damn it.

Comfort.

"Hey, that I can do. You want that fancy-pants cheese?" Okay, it was one thing for Artie to know where the cups were, but the frying pan? Either he was predictable or Artie was here more than he thought.

"No. I want the stuff with the crinkly plastic wrapper and white bread, and if you tell anyone else, I'll deny it. Alice and Mitch are being organic, and I said I'd try."

He could only be so good, and he felt like he had run a mile. Two. Underwater.

"Processed cheese food and gooey white bread fried with butter coming up." Soup can, pot, frying pan, can opener. Artie really was gonna make them grilled cheese and tomato soup. For breakfast. Damn.

Then he went and grabbed Artie a cherry cola and himself a cream soda. Cherry cola. He had cherry cola.

In his fridge.

He used a dishcloth to set Artie's on the table, open his, and pour it into a glass. No reason to beg for trouble, his brain was blown right open today.

"Thanks." Before long he had four neatly cut triangles of oozy cheesy bread and a bowl of an-orange-not-found-in-nature soup. "There you go. Eat up."

"Thank you." He waited for Artie to sit, and he did eat, and it was delicious and comforting, soothing. "This is just what the doctor ordered."

"Excellent." Man, Artie slurped his soup. That shouldn't surprise him. Didn't surprise him. "Been a long day."

"Tell me what happened?" He nibbled, leaning back in his chair. Artie wouldn't have bothered cooking if there wasn't something to say.

"Just a lot of crap. They grilled me and Leah about where we got the information to track Galloway down."

Galloway – big and Irish, hated women, hated cops, left a gun at one crime scene and Greg had held it. Actually traveled across Raleigh and held it, sitting in the passenger's seat of Artie's Camaro. He hated holding guns. Hated all the layers upon layers of things there.

"Ah. Your boss--" He never could remember if Frank Walters was a captain or if that was just television eating his brain. "—always seems to be concerned about me."

"Well, he figures I can't drag you to court." Dabbing a dribble, Artie sighed. "Leah's pregnant."

He tilted his head, sandwich half up to his mouth. Pregnant. Huh. "No wonder she looks tired. Does she... Will she still work?"

"Up to a point. The docs think she might have trouble. She's got the high blood pressure you know?" Leaning back, Artie rubbed the back of his neck. "She's just over three months; they think she'll work until five or six."

"Is Tim happy?" Artie wasn't happy; Greg wasn't surprised. Policemen liked things that stayed the same.

"He's over the fucking moon. And giving me the evil eye every time I come around." Yeah, Artie and Leah had never been together-together, but cops had a bond. That had to be hard.

He supposed.

"Protective? Tim? I might have to see that with my own eyes." He drank deep, washing down the last bit of sandwich. "Do you have to get a new partner, while she's gone?"

He was beginning to relax, feel the synapses in his brain ease, lose that white-hot sensitivity.

"No. At least when Amy over in Dan's precinct went on maternity leave, he didn't get anyone." As Greg relaxed, Artie got wound up, fingers drumming on the bar.

Weird how that worked. He wondered if the energy in the room did it or if they were simply diametrically opposed. "Good. I quite like her."

"Me, too." High praise for a man who usually grunted once for yes and twice for no.

He nodded, mind wandering, floating from thing to thing like a helium balloon in a high rise. Four years since the first phone call he'd made to the Raleigh PD. Four years since he'd gotten a sarcastic laugh and Artie'd grabbed his hand and snarled, "Psychic? Fucking prove it."

He had, too. Over and over and over and -- "Do you ever want children? A family?" he asked idly.

"Me?" That snapped him back. Artie looked absolutely horrified. "No way, man."

He laughed, amused balls to bones. "Don't sound so shocked. It is a biological imperative."

"Yeah? I missed the memo." The cherry cola can crumpled in Artie's fist. "I'm not the daddy type. Agatha's twins are plenty enough."

He nodded, shuddering. The one time Agatha had brought them to the shop had been... horrifying at best.

Artie gave him a keen look. "Better?"

"Yes. Yes, thank you." He met Artie's eyes straight on. "Are you going to want me to try the book again?"

He didn't want to. He would, if Artie was there, if Artie asked, but he didn't want to.

"Not now. Depends... you know?" That was one thing he *did* know. Once Artie had seen what it did to him, Artie'd believed. Well, the detective wasn't a cruel man, no matter what they said in the jail. "Right now, I'll take it, they'll run the blood, fingerprint it, check the envelope."

He nodded. "Just remember, it'll fade. The more people that touch it, the more it'll fade."

Although he wasn't sure it would, not with the blood and the fear on it. Not with the pain on it. Not with her on it.

"I know. I just, you've had enough for right now, man. Want me to do the dishes?"

"No. I will." He wanted to ask Artie to stay, but he knew. He could see the jitters, the way Artie's eyes shot to the elevator. "You want ice cream?"

"Sure. Sure. If you want." Yeah, Artie was a good guy. Annoying. But good. He could tell how much the man wanted to be gone, but he'd stay. A little longer, anyway.

And if he had chocolate almond in the refrigerator alongside his banana nut? Well, neither of them had to comment on it.

Chapter Two

Fuck, he was tired.

Artie got all three locks undone, foot stuck out to keep Duke from scrambling past him and down the stairs. Those college kids two flights down had just bought themselves a new little pit bull puppy, and sure as shit Duke'd kill it in a tussle. Beast.

Muscling through the stacks of this and piles of that, he managed to turn the police scanner off, turn the kitchen light on, and get his shoes off his feet, all at the same time. Artie plopped his stack of files down on the dinette table, ignoring it as it slid halfway off the cracked red vinyl, paper fluttering to the floor. The fridge yielded a beer and not much else, and he sighed, rubbing the back of his neck as Duke gnawed his ankle.

Damned fucking half-Siamese yowl. The cat looked just like John Wayne in *Rooster Cogburn*, and twice as fucking mean. It was hard to be mean back to a one-eyed cat.

"Looks like canned food for you tonight, buddy. And delivery for me."

His answering machine was empty, no blinking lights, no blinking number. Nothing.

Damn.

Looked like *he'd* have to call Greg. See how things were. Greg was always weird as hell the day after, and he'd want to know what Artie'd found out anyway.

What did it say that he had Greg on speed dial ahead of Domino's?

The phone rang and rang – one, two, come on Professor, three, four. It's not like the man was out and about wandering Lenoir Street. Right before the machine picked up, Greg did. "Hello? If you're selling something, be assured I'm not interested."

Man sounded tired, worn, ragged around the edges.

"I'm buying, Professor. What do you want me to pick up for supper?" That was that. He'd go see Greg, make sure for himself that everything was okay.

"Oh. Artie. Italian. Please." Greg never ate at restaurants, never, and take out could be challenging until the food was on Greg's plates. For a man that enjoyed food like Greg did, it was a shame. Hell, for a man that had lived a full life – dances, parties, department doo-dads – it was a tragedy. "I have a bottle of red."

"I'll go to Mario's." Mario's had the happiest chef in the world. He must have mistresses that wouldn't quit. "I'll be there in about thirty."

"The back door is unlocked." Greg hung up before he could bitch about being safe, not being stupid.

Fuck. One of these days some sicko would get to Greg that way. He called in an order for alfredo and that fancy assed cannelloni Greg liked, changed into jeans and a T-shirt, fed Duke (who growled at the canned shit), and headed out toward Pullen Park, the mid-October air crisp enough to justify the jacket that hid his holster.

Thirty minutes later exactly he let himself in at Greg's, taking the back steps two at a time.

The loft was spotless as usual, music low and almost unnoticeable – some jazz shit that managed not to be irritating. The heavy wood table was set, wine breathing – which was just a gross term, breathing. Who wanted their booze to breathe? Who actually set a table with cloth napkins, for God's sake? It was just unnatural that a single man should be so fucking neat, gay or otherwise.

"That you, Artie?"

"Yeah." Well, at least he wouldn't be horking up a hairball with supper. "I got you that rolled shit."

"Thank you. I made a salad to go with." Big-assed wooden bowl in too-long fingers, Greg was wearing a damn near see-through pair of pants, a loose tank top. Bare feet. No shaving that dark-dark stubble. Ah, twitchy today. He'd probably been naked all day.

Artie hoped the chef was having a damned good day.

"Cool. I got some of that bread if you want to get the olive oil. And that pepper grinder thing." He liked the freshly cracked pepper. Even if he would never admit it.

"Mmm... There are two pieces of cheesecake left, too, for after." Greg pottered, bare feet slapping on hardwood floors, as pristine white dishes filled with oil, with olives, with little chunks of white cheese.

The man did love his little dishes and fussy stuff. But it was good food and made things feel... well, special was a foofy sort of thought, but Artie wasn't gonna bitch. He slipped off his jacket, got out of his holster, and set it aside. Then Artie put the food out, got it on the plates, carefully, and let Greg get the bread. "You get any rest?"

"Not particularly. I got online, did some research. I was curious about the book. Did you?" His wine was poured, dark, dark red casting a shadow on the table.

"No." He stared at the wine. "The lab has the book. We're making zip headway on the missing person. Leah might have a bead on the blonde thing, though. She thinks she might have a couple of random disappearances."

Greg sat, dark head bowed almost like he was praying. Then black-as-pitch eyes met his, dead-on, shadows dark underneath them. There was a painting behind Greg on the stark white wall, a depiction of Dante's Inferno with horned beasts and fire and winged demons framing Greg's head. Even creepier was that Artie knew the backdrop behind him was dripping with cherubs and angels, the hosts of heaven hung on a blood red wall. Nothing like a sense of irony. "Let's eat. It smells too good to waste."

"You bet." The man was all skin and bones as it was. They could talk after. "Eat hearty."

The sauce on his pasta was perfect, and Greg moaned over his cannelloni. They fought over chunks of bread, flicked olives at each other, poured one glass of wine after another. Even the salad was perfect, both of them devouring it. The habit was threatening to become a tradition, the wine and the food and the idle chatter about movies and books and Duke.

"You know I'm gonna have to take him that white tuna stuff. He's pissed at me." Two nights in a row with no Swanson fried chicken? Oh, yeah. Duke was gonna piss on his bed for sure.

"Tuna's bad for him. He'll get crystals in his urine." Oh, no. No biological professor urine bullshit talk at he table.

"That's gross. And sorry, but he's too damned tough for anything like that." Oh, those olives were good. Green and salty. Almost squeaking in his teeth.

"He is a hard old bastard. You're well-suited. Hand me some bread." Greg could hold his liquor in that way that rare, super-tall, super-skinny men had, eyes as sharp and quick now as they'd been at the beginning of the bottle.

He tossed over a slice, heavy on the crust like Greg liked it, using his own to mop up the rest of his white sauce. God, that was a heart attack on a plate, but Mario's made it taste like heaven would be worth it. Artie figured he'd had enough of the damned wine that he might have to crash out in the Professor's front room.

"So nothing showed up in the mail today, right?"

"I didn't check." Greg shrugged, the motion deceptively casual. "Alice and Mitch watched the store today."

"Oh. Well, good." He'd go check later. Alice would have left it on the counter; she had been the first person to pull him aside, point out that Raleigh PD or not? Proof or not? Bullshit or not? The Professor was the real deal. He looked Greg over, noting the tapping fingers and twitchy mouth. "What else?"

"For someone who swears not to be psychic, you always know." Greg looked over, shook his head.

"No, I just read body language. And you're vibrating." The bread had a nice crust on it that was just perfect for that last noodle to stick to. "Did you say cheesecake?"

"I did. Chocolate." Greg stood up, grabbing two plates from the refrigerator. "Alice's mother made it. It's good."

He hid a grin in his wine glass. "Maybe you should make coffee. And it's not gonna get you out of telling me."

"Someone would think you were a detective, the way you ask questions." The coffee pot was started with a touch, Greg beginning to flutter again. A nightmare maybe, or something Greg remembered.

"Sit. Tell me. You'll need the chocolate after." Yeah. That look, the haunted one, flashed across that narrow face. Damn.

Greg sat beside him, long body settling easily in the high backed chair, leg thrumming. "I... I heard him. I could hear him telling her about things. About what he wanted to do. He wants to do things to them. Then I heard more. About me. He told her about me."

Oh, fuck a duck. "What did he say, Greg? What does he know?"

"He knows I'm here. He told her about the copper pyramid in the shop. The one that Cat Peterson made for me. About how he was going to leave bits of her here. About how I look when I sleep." Those eyes stared at him, into him. Not even seeing him anymore. "Tell me I have an overactive imagination, Artie. Tell me I'm just spooked, because this time the evidence came to me."

Damned if he didn't wish he could. But this guy was already fitting the kind of psycho profile that would do exactly what Greg had described. He reached out for Greg's hands, stopping right before their skin met.

"I don't know, Greg. I...I think we can't be too careful. You're gonna start locking that door."

"Unless you're coming up with Italian, it's a deal." He almost laughed. A deal until Greg started working or reading and forgot. A deal until somebody said the right series of things and whatever it was in the Professor's mind that fired wrong went batshit crazy and Greg did… Who the hell knew what.

The man was a menace to himself. "Okay. And I'll have a uniform pass by every so often. Make it a known presence."

"You don't have to. The neighbors cluck their teeth and get all paranoid."

"What neighbors, Doc? The tattoo parlor on the corner? The bead shop next door? This isn't Hayes Barton." He could hear Greg's bare feet tapping on the wood floor, and it was enough to drive a sane man batty. "It's going to happen. Cope. Tell me more and don't worry about the roaming flatfoots."

Greg steepled his fingers, chewing on his lip. "The book isn't rare, particularly. It had layered drawings of musculature, veins, skeletal systems. It wasn't exact by modern standards, but it was what physicians had."

"Had when? When did they use a book like that?" Something was niggling at him. Something that teased the crime film historian in him.

"Late nineteenth century. 1880-1892. I don't have the publication date, so I used the title. *Greune's Physician Guide.*"

"But you don't think it was a reprint?" The lab never told him squat. He always had to send Leah, and she'd been in Missing Persons all day. It would help had he not sort of threatened the little shit that ran DNA over the Bigger's case. Still, rules got broken where kids were involved. Damn it.

"It could have been. It seemed old. It was from a library, wasn't it? Hundreds of people touched it. Hundreds before he did."

"It was, yeah." That much he knew. It had stamps and labels inside it. One of those pockets. "They think it was cleaned out in a book sale. When they cleared out the outdated books. They're working on seeing what library it was, but it's all blacked out with black marker."

"Shit. I was hoping it would be easy, you know? Library card. Address. Bad guy. Little blonde reunited with her parents. Happy ending." Greg stood, pacing a little, going to look at the heaven picture, all dark and haunted in comparison with the blue-eyed blondes on the canvas.

"No. Sorry, man." Time for cheesecake. Artie put the dishes in the sink and started cutting. "Is that homemade raspberry sauce?"

"Yes. The delivery from the farmer's market came. I got too many raspberries to eat on my own." Greg moved slowly, distracted, distant.

They passed as Greg got plates down, and Artie let his fingers brush Greg's shirt, just barely, assuring himself the guy was really there. It seemed like he was a galaxy away. "I like raspberries."

"Yeah, but not blueberries. They give you hives."

He blinked. He couldn't remember ever telling... Yeah. "They do. And oranges make me itch."

Greg nodded, pulling out the coffee cups, the sugar, the white mugs almost disappearing on the white stone countertops. "There's something about orange juice that clears my head. I think I'd drink it even if it made me itch."

"It's good for you. I like grape juice." Well. That was banal. The coffee stopped perking and he poured, the brew rich and dark, clearing his head. "Look, that wine was hefty. You mind if I hang out a bit?"

"Of course not. Your chair is free, always." His chair, the comfortable, deep, charcoal one with the heavy quilt over it. He'd never seen Greg sit in it. Of course, he'd only made the mistake of sitting on the long white sofa once before Greg had explained.

Well, yelled, more than explained.

He'd never done that again. The chair had an ottoman, or what he called a footstool, and was almost as comfy as a bed. "Cool. Just let me call Leah and let her know where I'll be."

Greg nodded and started on the dishes. "I'll bring the coffee and sweet. You set up the backgammon board."

That he could do. Even if he did have to fight the urge to take the cheesecake with him. Greg liked to do. And if he could do even something as small as make a nice tray to put on the coffee table, so be it. Artie called his partner, got settled, got the board going, smiling at Greg as he came over.

"Now, no cheating this time, detective. We'll share the dice and I'll know." Greg put the tray beside them, long legs curling up under him as he settled. The jazz changed to something like bluegrass, but not quite.

"I didn't cheat." Maybe he knocked a piece to a different sliver of board, but hey, he had big hands.

"Of course not. You? Are honest as the day is long. You can go first." Man, sugar wouldn't melt in that man's mouth.

It did him no good to let his thoughts linger on Greg's mouth, though. Especially if they were going to be touching the same things. That was a thought for late at night, sprawled in his bed, when even Duke couldn't see. He took the first move, getting several pieces in play.

Greg rolled well, rebutting easily. They'd played on this board a hundred times, maybe more, drinking coffee and bantering like old men.

It was hard to believe, sometimes, that they'd known each other as long as they had. The cheesecake went down easy, the chocolate dark and smooth, the raspberries just biting. "So did you ever fix that thing with the distributors or whatever?"

Greg laughed. "Alice did. You should have seen her screaming and throwing things at the poor rep. I quite enjoyed the show. So much for peace-and-new-age-light. That woman? Is all about the profit margin."

Oh, Christ. Alice was a harridan when it came to Greg and twice as bad when it came to the store.

"Yeah? She's got brass balls, that one." The round little redhead had come after him once in the very beginning, after he'd dragged Greg down to the station and they'd ended up calling an ambulance for the guy. Christ, Greg had been convulsing, flailing around on the ground like a landed fish. She'd come down that hospital corridor like a flash of light, all teeth and claws, and so damned loud that Artie'd wanted to curl up and whimper. He'd deserved it. "You ever wonder why it is the women are so good at shit like that?"

"Must be the maternal instinct. My mother could scream like a banshee." Greg bumped one of his pieces, smiling. "How about Leah? Do you ever let her play bad cop?"

"She doesn't really have to." The woman had a way. Quiet. Just staring. "She has that natural guilt factor. They start babbling."

Greg chuckled low. The professor and Leah had a healthy respect for each other; she'd been faster to believe Greg than Artie had, even if she'd never been able to get an iota of info from the man in babble mode. "I can believe that. Although you're the one who always gets me. Always."

"You don't need what Leah has. You need pushing. But just the right way. Someone who knows what questions to ask." His teeth clicked together as he bit off all sorts of stupid shit.

Greg nodded, rolled the dice, and groaned. "Even when I don't want to hear and you're cursing my dice rolls."

"Me?" He raised a brow. "Now, you know I would never wish you ill, not even in backgammon."

"Not even toward the end of the..." Greg tilted his head, blinked. "Did you hear something?"

Artie stopped, listened, slowing his breathing to hear. "No. Did you?"

Greg nodded, standing up and heading for the rickety old elevator that the fire marshal should have condemned twenty-five years ago. "I think I did. I should go and look."

"No!" The man had not a lick of sense. "You stay out of that elevator." Heaving up out of his chair, Artie grabbed his jacket and yanked his pistol out. "Stay. I'll go check."

"It's my shop. I'm going with you. It's probably Alice, forgetting her thermos." Greg even looked like he knew he was lying. Stubborn bastard. Oh. Oh, that was the door. Damn it.

"Then stay behind me and don't get in my way. And we take the stairs." If someone had gotten in meaning harm, that damned elevator could be a menace. One way or the other, it was a dead giveaway that they were coming. Artie headed down, slow and easy, letting his eyes adjust to the gloom.

Greg jittered along behind him, bare feet padding on the stairs, hand sliding on the rail. Always moving, always making noise.

Damn it. At the foot of the stairs he stopped, holding up a hand for Greg to be still. He searched the dark, trying to make out distinct shapes. Books, shelves, counter, register, leaning card table with Mitch's tarot cards. Wind chimes, crystals, that stupid fucking pyramid. Man, the whole place reeked of incense. Mitch must have been here all day.

He could feel Greg vibrating, shivering, hand reaching for the lights. He made a soft noise, knocking Greg's hand away. Not yet. Not until he had checked all of the danger areas. Ceiling, corners, doors, floors, right? Cautiously, slowly, he stepped down into the back of the shop, seeing nothing. No darker shadows, nothing moving. The pyramid, though. There was something there.

A small package wrapped in brown paper, not big enough to be a pipe bomb, almost inconsequential.

Weird.

Too fucking weird.

The shop phone rang, making Greg jump, curse and step back, move toward the light switch again.

He let Greg go this time, heading for the door to see how the deliverer of the package had got in, closing his eyes a split second before the light went on so he wouldn't be blinded. The lights flooded the store, dozens of crystals catching the light and sending rainbows everywhere. Adorable.

Greg headed for the phone, barking out a hello and then going silent. The door had been popped, the ancient lock pretty well hanging out of the jamb. But as bad as the wood was, it might not even have made a noise. No matter how much he lectured, Greg and Alice just kept talking about the damned historical value, the beauty of the handiwork. It just wasn't worth this sort of risk and…

Greg's voice, low and stressed, pushed into his attention. "…understand. No. No, I won't ignore the mail again. There's no reason to escalate things." Greg was staring at the counter, scribbling furiously, the man gone as white as that damned sofa upstairs.

He propped some kind of South American shamanistic mystic fertility walking stick under the busted door to hold it closed and went over, staring over Greg's shoulder.

"Him. He's watching. Says to open the mail when it comes. He's watching. Deep voice, rough. Raw."

Wheeling, he checked windows, going over the whole perimeter. There was no one close, so he automatically started scanning likely spots outside where someone could watch with binoculars or a scope. The street was pretty quiet; it was too early for the tattoo crowd.

"Yes. I understand. No. I... I understand. I'll try harder to hear what you're trying to tell me." Greg walked over toward the pyramid, staring down at the package. "No. No, I haven't opened it yet. I just came... I just came downstairs..."

Oh, Jesus. The guy was still on the phone. Still. He needed to get these lines tapped. He needed to get Greg away from there. Away from the windows. No way was Greg opening the package with the freak talking in his ear. Overload for sure. He'd just have to grab it.

Greg didn't reach for the little package, though; he went for the front door, for the doorknob, head jerking back with a snap as his long fingers closed around the metal. "White truck. Little. Dented. She hurt your hand. She bit your hand. I can see your hands."

His gut tightened, bile rising as all he could do was wait and see what happened next. Remember what happened. Goddamn, he hated being useless.

He couldn't call in the uniforms until the call was over. Not if they really wanted to know what Greg had to say.

"Fuck you, too. You coward. You come back here for me if you can. I can see you. You have a doll in there. Tools. A... a...a cheap watch." Greg was beginning to shake, the man hitting his knees with a sharp crack, the phone sliding across the tile, plastic shattering and scattering about.

"Shit!" On his knees in a flash, Artie was touching Greg without even thinking about it, holding the man up when he would have crumpled.

Greg jerked, eyes flying open, hands tearing free from the doorknob and holding his face. "Raspberries. You like raspberries because they're tart."

"Yeah. They go good with chocolate." He squeezed Greg's upper arms, supporting him, letting him know Artie was there and the psycho wasn't. Thin. Fuck, the man was thin, but strong.

"Yes. Yes. Raspberries and chocolate and coffee and your chair all together. Like home." Greg nodded, fingers exploring his face, just touching him, cheeks and eyebrows and jaw.

It had to be the weirdest fucking thing that had ever happened to him...something he'd been hoping for the longest time, but under the worst circumstances. He woulda laughed had it actually been funny. Artie chafed Greg's skin, feeling goose bumps.

"Uh-huh. You kicking my ass at backgammon. Alfredo. It's a tradition, man."

Greg nodded, relaxing a little, eyes closing. "Yes. Yes. Our tradition. We'll have to replace the doorknob. This one's poisoned."

"Not to mention broken. We'll do it, but I have to get someone out here first. They're gonna have to sweep the place, man." That was gonna kill Greg, he knew. He'd keep the crew to a minimum, but people would still have to touch Greg's stuff.

"No." Those black eyes met his, that familiar, heart wrenching panic right there. "They'll be thinking, Art. Over and over and over. They'll be everywhere."

"I know. I know, man, and I'm sorry. Leah can come. And we can try to get one processor. You know? But we have to collect what we can." He'd do as much of the work as he could. He would. And it was just the shop, just Greg's public face.

Greg nodded. "I know. I know you will. You take care of me." Greg pursed thin lips, fingers just brushing his mouth. "You do."

"I do." Greg had become like his personal fucking mission in life somewhere between that first case, where he'd called into the station and said he knew who'd killed that society wench, and now. It was fucking odd. "You know I will if I can."

"They can't come into the stairwell. They have to stay in the store." Greg's head tilted. "He was driving away in a truck. He said he was watching us. He said he knew I hadn't opened the mail. How did he know that?"

"I don't know. We'll make sure there's nothing planted. Okay? He could have just had binoculars. Come on, Greg. Let's go upstairs so I can call." He wanted Greg out, away from that damned box before they opened it, away from the windows for fuck's sake.

"Your people won't let me read the box, if they come first." Greg stood with him and it meant something that Greg would touch it, even though the man was shaken and sick and scared. Even if those eyes begged him to say no, it wasn't necessary. All it would take was a word from him and Greg would do it.

"No, and I don't want you to." He sighed, shook his head. "But you're supposed to. It's part of his game, and if he's leaving you clues..."

"Okay. Okay." Greg stumbled toward the pyramid, the copper tubing soldered with silver. "Might as well just dive in. You take notes; I'll talk as long as I can."

"Wait. Wait, let me get you something. Orange juice. Something." Artie caught up, caught Greg's arm. The man was just gonna fall over.

"God, that feels good." Greg squeezed his fingers, gave a near hysterical laugh. "Details, details, detective. Take notes. It'll be fast."

Then, sure as shit, Greg reached into the pyramid and picked the little brown paper package up. All he could do now was listen and try to record every fucking detail. They'd been here before.

Artie hated every minute of it.

"Underground. Red lights. Swinging red lights. Scalpels. The knife is to scare them. The rest is worse. Worse. The rest is work. Katy. Karen. Kaitlin. K. Her name has a K and her granny gave her a necklace when she was twelve. She screamed and screamed and he made her stop. Dripping. The blood is dripping. She's put in the box. A box with the others. There's water. His boots never get wet. Never."

The notebook and pen felt like it weighed about eighty pounds, but Artie got it all, writing in his own sort of shorthand. All the while he listened for outside noises and watched Greg's face as it got paler and paler.

Greg didn't open the package, just held it, rocking it as if comforting someone. "Kathy or Karen or Kari, and she was a street kid, young enough to be scared. A throwaway person. A hole. She stopped being frightened at the end. She went home to the mountains and he screamed and tore at her and she didn't care and her eyes were green but they're not anymore and there's part of her in here, in this box and I can't open it but she's in here, too and..." The words trailed off, murmured lost nonsense. Greg was wandering, eyes rolling.

Artie dropped the pen and paper and caught Greg with one hand, taking the box away with the other. Part of her in there. Jesus. He set the box aside on the table, trying to touch as little of its surface as possible. "Come on, man. Let's go up now. Let's get some juice in you and sit down and all."

"Orange juice makes you itch and you're allergic to blueberries."

Leading Greg back upstairs, Artie nodded, talking in a low voice. "And I like raspberries and chocolate, but my favorite is banana splits. They always make me think of when I was a kid and I still thought cops were heroes who always got their man." One more step, then another. "And you like orange juice and cream puffs, but not together, because that's like orange juice and toothpaste. Icky."

"Yes." Greg followed him, shuffling like a hypnotized man. "Yes, and your grandfather wore a badge and it was shiny and you watched it. His eyes were the same gray as yours."

His breath caught in his chest. Yeah. Yeah, his grandfather had been his damned hero. He'd never even told his dad that. "Come on. Come and sit." There. Down on the couch, and he left Greg hugging himself as he went to the kitchen and got juice, finally digging his cell out.

"Hey. Hey, honey. Look, yeah, I know it's late. It's -- Yeah. Another box. Can you come? And we want someone good. Maybe Dave or Laura. Okay. Yeah. Bye."

Bless Leah's heart. She was a trooper.

"Here, man, drink up." Greg had shifted to the gray chair -- his chair – was curled in it, wrapped in the quilt, looking lost. Goddamn. Artie plopped down on the ottoman thingee. "Come on, Greg. You gotta drink or you'll pass out. And that'll suck. Then you'll dream."

"No dreams." Greg drank the juice down, long throat working. "No dreams."

"No. No dreams." Mind racing, he sat and waited for Leah, rubbing Greg's leg with one hand. The doorknob, the street outside, the pyramid... yeah. God, Greg looked like crap. "Have some more. Do you want a sandwich?"

"No. She'll be here soon. I'll wait here for you to be finished." Greg cuddled into the quilt, moaning softly. "I'll wait here."

"Okay." He patted Greg's knee. "Okay. Everything will be okay."

He only hoped he was telling the truth.

If there was one thing he never wanted to do to Greg, it was lie.

***

Greg could hear them downstairs. It was a mixture of Artie snapping out orders and some -- two? Three? -- women answering. It wasn't impossible; people touched things all the time -- customers, Alice, Mitch. It was just hard enough to have a place that he could relax down there; now, people would touch his little chair, his office, move the little boxes of plastic gloves he kept so he could count money and shelve books.

Okay. Stop. They weren't coming upstairs. He was safe. Safe and not acting like a dipshit. He knew how the bad episodes went, how the paths in his head felt open and raw, open for the tiniest bit of information.

He just had to remind himself that he survived the very first episode, back when any touch made him scream, back when Jeff had signed for the doctors to administer Lithium, Thorazine, enough Flexeril to leave him unable to hold his head up, walk. He'd survived that.

He could handle a little police investigation, no sweat.

He walked down the steps, leaning hard against the wall, to deadbolt the door. Artie had an elevator key, once they were all finished, and no one would get up into his space. Touch his home.

Of course, climbing up the thrice-damned stairs took forever, and he made the last five steps on hands and knees.

"You could have just called, Greg." Oh. Alice. Round and familiar, her hands helping him to a standing position. She was aggravated that the police were messing with things, had called to have the door replaced tonight, and had called the insurance. Artie'd sent her up to check on him.

Artie lied.

This was ridiculous -- the whole thing was just ridiculous. Here he was, a full-grown man -- a fucking Ph.D., for Christ's sake – gagging and swaying, leaning on one soft 100%-pure cotton-clad shoulder that could more than bear his weight across his living room rug.

"If you're kicking yourself, stop. You'll just start throwing up." Alice settled him on the sofa, started cleaning up coffee cups and plates, carefully shifting the backgammon game aside.

"You're mother henning."

Pale blue eyes caught him, worried and fond all at once. "Yes, it's my job. Artie's worried about you."

"Yes, and you're worried about the shop."

"My shop is fine. I'll come in early-early with Mitch. He'll help me clean." She sighed, looked down. "I want you to stay out of the office for a few days, okay?"

"Artie?" If it was Artie, he could handle it.

She shook her head. "No. Miss Leah. She got sick. I think she's pregnant; she carries herself like she is."

"Yeah?" He should tell Artie. Leah should know that people knew, just in case. He leaned back against the sofa, sighed.

"You want to go up to the roof, honey? The jasmine's not all gone yet."

He shook his head. No, he didn't want to play up there, not right now. Even if it was the best place, the reason he bought the building. His garden. The sky.

"Okay. I'm going to go see if they need me and then get home, doctor up Mitch's hand. That cut from the dumpster's just not wanting to heal." Cut hand. Greg frowned, then shook his head. No, not cut. Bit. The K girl had bitten... him. Alice poured him a cup of coffee, made him toast, kept jabbering, kept talking on and on and on as she disappeared, locking the back door behind her.

Oh. Better.

It wasn't perfect; he could hear them, but it was better. Touching Alice's books and opening and closing the door. The scratch as they moved the pyramid.

It was maddening, and if it hadn't been Artie and Leah down there, he wouldn't have allowed it. He wasn't sure if Leah should be down there. What if someone saw her? Hurt the baby? Hurt Artie?

It wasn't the urge to help that got him moving, as much as he'd like to think it was. No, it was the phone ringing, over and over, shrill and loud, drilling into him. The sound stopped as his answering machine kicked on, then began again.

He levered himself off the couch and onto the floor, heading to bury himself beneath Gran's quilt, on Artie's chair. He simply ignored the noise, the music, the pain in the back of his forehead.

Think, Greg. Focus.

Gran's voice.

Art's laugh.

Gran's tea, spicy and orangey and sweet.

Art's watch, it had been Art's grandfather's.

He had no idea how long he sat on the floor, his head on Artie's chair, before the store beneath went quiet and the elevator started up, creaky and groaning. It had best be Artie. If it was a psycho killer, he'd probably offer up his throat.

"Hey." Artie. It was Artie kneeling in front of him. "You wanna sit *in* the chair, man?"

"I thought about it, but it's really a bit of a climb." Artie looked stressed out, tired, eyes bruised and shadowed. The sun was trying to come up, to fill the room with a pink light. "How'd it go down there?"

"It went. It's a shop. People touch stuff. We've got about a million prints, but I doubt there's a usable one. The box..." Artie trailed off, shaking his head. Giving him plenty of time to protest, Artie reached for him, grabbing him under the armpits and hauling him up, plopping him in the chair.

"What was in the box?" His head rolled, surrounded by safety, by family. By Artie. He loved this chair.

"You were right. It was a piece of someone. Your girl, most like. We're gonna try and ID her. I need something to eat. And maybe a stiff shot."

"I have your whiskey in the wet bar." He could stand up and cook. He could. At least he was fairly sure he could. Mostly. "You want eggs and toast?"

He wouldn't fuck up eggs and toast.

"That sounds good. Real good." Artie sat on the ottoman, elbows on his knees, head down. "Goddamn, I hate this."

He nodded, looking at the different colors in Artie's hair. Some were almost white, some a real gold. A shiny gold. Funny wasn't it? The things you focused on? The things you saw?

He reached out, braced himself for the rush of visuals and sounds when his hands stroked through Artie's hair.

Tired. Mainly Artie was just really damned tired. The rest was a blur. Leah. The pyramid, over and over. A bloody scrap of finger wrapped in cream paper – gift wrapped. Artie leaned into the touch, humming.

God, it felt good. Warm. He kept touching, breathing nice and slow. Eventually the pyramid would go away. It had to. Just relax, Artie. Let it go away.

"Feels good. I told Leah to call me when she gets home. Not sure where my phone is." The image faded slowly, but it faded. Then it was just Leah with a big old belly and swollen ankles and Artie fluttering around like a nervous hummingbird.

He smiled. Oh, yeah, Artie as hummingbird. Duke wouldn't have any of that. His touch moved down, working the deltoids gently. If Artie didn't know, Greg wouldn't either.

"Mmm. Damn." Oh, that helped. He could feel the tight muscles release, could feel Artie sink down. The old ottoman creaked and groaned, sliding a little, bringing Artie closer.

He nodded, eyes closing. It had been so long since he'd been able to just touch and not be scared. So long.

Like three thousand five hundred and seventy three days long.

Artie's eyes popped open, searching him. "You're touching me."

"Do you want me to stop?" Greg hoped Artie didn't ask him to stop. Not yet. Five more minutes and he'd go make eggs. Bacon. Souffle. Anything.

"No." Those eyes looked like storm clouds. Okay, so that was a cliché from hell, but there it was. "No, it feels good."

"Yes. It does." So Greg kept doing it, letting the wonder and awe of really and truly touching someone wash the horrors of the night away. Artie's shoulders were hard, firm, hot under his hands. Not even murder could supersede this, right here, right now.

There was nothing coming through now but warm. Artie just leaned against him and let him work away every bit of stiff and worried and scared.

Oh. For this he would even make omelets. Frittatas. Crepes.

Greg rested his cheek against Artie's head, sighing softly. At peace.

Half turning, Artie put an arm around him, holding him loosely, sitting quiet.

"Do you still want eggs?" His fingers explored Artie's, curious. There was a scar there, a little bump here.

"Hmm?" The cheek against his belly was stubbled and rough, rubbing as Artie turned his head a little more. "Oh, sure. Whatever."

He smiled. Artie didn't want eggs. Artie was happy where he was, except... Greg frowned, fingers searching out a sore spot on Artie' neck, rubbing. "Better?"

"Uh-huh. Oh, good." They sort of...oozed. Artie scooted and pulled and pushed, and the next thing he knew they were both sitting in the chair, sort of squashed.

He just moaned, drew the quilt over them both. Artie fluttered against him, and he nodded. "You're fine. Stay. This is good."

"Okay. Okay, sure." Artie stayed. Right there. Happy as anything. He could tell that by the smile.

The jazz started up again on the CD player. Artie liked it well enough, for jazz.

"Don't worry. The Celtic stuff you like better is next." Greg closed his eyes, fingers moving and searching, even after they were both asleep.

Chapter Three

He's made an impact.

Interesting, to watch the professor walk up and down the stairs in the back, so careful not to touch the wall, the stairway, anything. So interesting to see the long fingers wrapped in plastic gloves, taking a book off a shelf and handing it, so carefully, to a wide-eyed, stammering customer.

A pretty customer.

She's not collectible, but part of him wants to reach out, grab her perfectly manicured little hand holding a pointless book on love potions and aphrodisiacs, and slice deep into the skin. Take that wrist and rub it over the professor's face, drip blood in those eyes, in his mouth, make him scream and sob and drown in it.

It's a pretty fantasy. The idea of watching the man writhe and groan, of seeing the stains ruin the pristine white sweater. Such a pretty thought.

Still, the time isn't right, and he wants to know, needs to know, really. Needs to know how worried he should be.

He slips out of the shop, nodding at the fat woman who always gets the mail and watches the professor like a hawk, smiling at her, and waiting patiently for her smile in return. The garbage cans are in the back and he takes a cloth from his pocket. He'd used it, only this morning, hand moving furiously as he listened to the tapes he has – five tapes, four sweet, dear screams, one deep, genteel cultured voice.

The garbage goes out every night. Every night before the professor heads up. He slides the cloth over the handle, his thumb swollen and aching, throbbing as he rubs himself over the galvanized steel. See what this tells you. See if you can see me.

After all, the collection needs to be protected at all costs.

***

They didn't say a word about it.

Artie just wasn't sure if he was happy or pissed.

Three days later they still had no leads on the girl, on the blood -- hers or the stuff on the book -- and no fucking prints except for one serial shoplifter Greg could watch out for now.

Greg opened the mail religiously, but nothing new came. Hell, even Alice knew what to look for. Artie figured the guy must be choosing his next victim, just out there, on their streets. It chafed like a bad pair of jeans. Damn it.

"What have you got for me, babe?" Poor Leah. She looked so tired.

There were papers everywhere, scribbled on, drawn on. Every fucking angle that they could see together. And they didn't have a motherfucking thing. "Bupkes."

"Shit. There's got to be something, honey." There had to be. He nodded to a couple of guys that passed by, vice detectives if he remembered right. "What about all those missing persons files?"

Leah leaned across the desk, tugged the files over. "Okay, stud. Here goes. There's been thirty-five verified missing persons in the city so far this year. I got six under twenty-five, blonde runaways. Three with K names – Kathy Miller, Karen Herschfeld and a… Kathleen Boule." Six pretty girls – from scary young to hard-bitten -- stared up at him.

"Okay, so that's something, at least. Do we have any uniforms to do some footwork, or are we on our own?"

She arranged shit like that. He just dug like a terrier.

"Cap gave me Trewwater and Vargas. They're on the families, last knowns, all that. Aggie's working the finger we got. You know how she is. She won't give up a single fucking breath until the whole job's done."

"Yeah, and in the meantime I have a witness who's jumping out of his skin at every noise." Greg fucking worried him. He was just fading, like.

"The professor needs a standing 'scrip for Valium. Nothing else has come?" Two books -- one old one on surgery, one new one about head injuries and mental illness, both splashed with blood matching the finger, and stagnant water. The finger, conveniently missing a print. That was it. Still, he'd bet Greg had stopped sleeping in the bed. Again.

"Not that I know of. I'm heading over in a bit, just to look around." Look around, check on Greg, maybe play backgammon.

Leah nodded, curls bobbing as she started sorting through papers again. "I printed a bunch of knife photos and truck makes to show him, that sort of thing. He's locking his doors, recording phone calls still?"

"He is." He'd damned well better be. "I'll take them with me."

The last thing he really wanted was to talk to Greg about the case, but they weren't talking on other stuff.

"Oh, that bitch reporter? Uh… Denice Powers. The one that blew his cover? She's been sniffing, along with that little blonde one. Uh. Ginny. Georgette. Something." Leah got that look, sharp and fierce, the one that he knew meant trouble. "I'm thinking she might have heard from our guy, to know to be asking questions already."

Nodding, he sat back, his back cracking. "Fuck a duck."

He'd kill her if she got Greg hurt. His brow furrowed. That was a fierce feeling, one he'd tuck away and look at later.

"Could be nothing. Most likely is. Still, it's a reason to poke a little." Leah pushed her hair back, rubbing her forehead, chewing on her lips. "Tell me, man. Why now? Why'd he surface? We got no bodies, we got nothing until he starts playing cat and mouse with the doc. What's he want?"

"I don't know, babe, but it's pissing me off. You need to go home. Get some rest." She needed to sit and get off her fucking feet. Let Tim give her a massage. Get away from all this death and blood. It couldn't be good for the baby.

Leah nodded, handed him a sheaf of papers. "I know you don't want to hear it, but it's only a matter of time before we have to dig on the professor's background, just to see who could hold this kind of focus, who wants to screw him."

Artie sighed. "I know, babe. I know." Hoisting up out of his chair, he grabbed his jacket. "Come on. I'll walk you out."

She buttoned up, grabbed her own work from the desk.

Rick passed by, winking at him, mischief written all over the man's face. "Man, our favorite lady's getting puffy. I'm thinking she'll be cute as all hell in a little pink polka-dotted maternity dress."

"Suck my swollen ass, Garcia. Give me three minutes on the training mat with you and you'll be begging to wear the dress." She made a fake swipe for Rick's nuts and the man hooted, heading down to the Captain's office with a pile of reports. Oh. Blah. Fucking reports. Typing. Printing. He'd rather gargle razor blades.

"Hello? Studmuffin? Artie?" Leah popped his arm, shaking her head. "You're getting as bad as the professor. We're going to Chi-Chi's tonight. Come with us. Have guacamole and a beer or two. Duke can wait for his tuna."

"Thanks, honey, but you and Tim go ahead. He's getting grumpier about me encroaching on your time." He frowned. "And no beer for you."

"Spoilsport." Leah stuck her tongue out, punched the button for the elevator. "Tell the doc hey for me and to take it easy."

"I will." She smelled like baby powder and hot tea as he bent to kiss her cheek. "And you enjoy. See you tomorrow."

Duke could wait for his tuna for sure. He was an independent thinker. Hell, Artie figured Duke could open tuna cans on his own; he just liked for Artie to feel useful. Greg was more important.

His cell rang as he got the key in the door of his Camaro, jiggling it to make the damn thing pop the lock. Not that she wasn't worth a little shake and jiggle, but once in a while it'd be nice to... "Yeah."

"Detective? I'm sorry to bother you." It took him a second to follow along with the soft, gentle voice on the other end of the line. "...wife said this would be the number to contact you on. It's on the store rolodex."

"Yeah." Uh... Mark. Mork. Mitch! "What's up, Mitch?" Goddamned fucking lock. There. He hopped in, his gut clenching up.

"Alice asked me to call. You see. Well, Greg seems to have, well... taken a walk." Which would be perfectly normal for every person on Earth but Dr. Greg Please No Crowds who never left home.

"Taken a..." The engine roared as he gunned it out. "He's not on the roof?"

As many God-forsaken plants as the man grew up there, it wasn't inconceivable that Greg could be hiding up there.

"I've been up there twice and in the storage on the third floor. I even looked in the tool shed. Alice is out searching for him in the few places he's been known to go – that little florists, the coffee shop on the corner that knows him. She's not back yet. Oh, wait. Did you?"

He heard a rustle, then Alice's voice was on the line, brassy and loud and tinged with worry. "He went to put the trash out. The trash bag's on the ground. The lid's off. He took his jacket. You know how he is, Artie. He's on the trail again."

"I'll be right there."

Jesus Christ. He hung up with Alice without another word, dialing Greg's cell. He was one of three people who had the number.

It rang and rang, and just before the voice mail picked up, Greg did. "Hello?"

"Hey." Breathing deep to calm himself, Artie hung a right, heading for the shop. "Where are ya?"

"Wandering. Walking. Avoiding raindrops and crowds. Trying to find where he was standing. He walked and walked and then he did something, something confusing. It's not working." No. No, he didn't imagine it was. Not with that so-fake calm tone in Greg's voice. "Are you still on duty?"

"No. I was on my way to see you. Mitch called. Where are you, man? I'll get you." Greg on a trail could be like a hound on a scent.

Not knowing how to get home.

"Mitch? I told them I'd be out for the evening. At least I thought I did. You'd think I wasn't a grown man." Greg sighed, the sound frustrated. "I know I'm close to something. I just know, you know? There's got to be something around here."

"Well, if there is, then you shouldn't find it alone, doofball. Tell me where you are. I promise not to turn the siren on."

Stubborn, fool man.

"Oh, God. No sirens. I'm at the corner of Atlantic and Sego." Christ, Greg'd been moving. "It's really getting to be autumn, isn't it?"

"It is. Gonna get crisp soon." Burning a u-ie, Artie doubled back on himself, flipping off the SUV that tried to cut him off. He'd catch up. And he needed to keep Greg talking. "So what are you following?"

"A tickle. An itch. I feel like an ant. Did you know they can find chemical trails that have been tracked over? I mean, if I thought I wouldn't lose it, I'd take off my shoes and stand here, but there's just too much traffic. You should come down here and eat, though. There are some neat looking places."

"I'm coming. We can get something, maybe." Not that Greg would eat in. They'd have to get take out, and then only after he'd checked out the containers. "Look, stay put, okay? No more wandering. Tell me why you headed that way."

"I took out the trash. I lifted the lid and he was on it. All over it like a stain, I could smell him. I needed to walk. I kept going back out there and finally got my jacket."

"The trash? Did you get anything from the lid? Even a little?" Damn traffic lights. Come on, come on. His gut was just churning. He needed to call Leah. Get Forensics to Greg's.

"Just his hands. The last girl hurt his hand. Bit him. It's got bacteria in it now."

Serve the bastard right if he rotted away. "From your trash? What is he doing in your trash, Greg?"

"I don't know. Looking? Daring me? What's in my trash?" Greg sighed, and Artie could almost see him rubbing the bridge of his nose.

"Your life. What you eat. Where you shop. Receipts." Fuck, any cop worth his salt knew what kind of evidence you could find in the trash. "Your head hurt?"

"Yeah. Yeah. Throbbing like a bitch. I need a cup of coffee in the worst way."

"Figured. You sound tired." He always asked, then distracted. Then asked some more. Greg could only do so much at a time. Nothing had ever scared him more than when Greg had lost it on him, eyes rolling up while that long body convulsed. Fuck. He'd honestly believed the man would stroke out. "I bet we can get you one of those really strong espressos with that milk stuff."

"Oh, yes. Caffeine is proof there is a benevolent deity and it adores us. What do you want for supper? I could go in somewhere and order. To go."

He thought about what Greg would like, would find comforting. "Hey, how about some kind of fried chicken. Maybe some mac and cheese. Something plebian. We can stop and get Krispy Kremes for dessert."

The hungry little groan he got made him laugh. Alice and Mitch and their macrobiotic, all-organic, tofu-loving ways would have a cat.

Hey. That was an idea. He should give them Duke for a week. They'd be eating grits with red-eye in no time. "Okay, I should be at your cross street in about five minutes. Look for soul food. Oh, and I want greens."

"And biscuits. We should have biscuits with it." The life was back in that voice, the focus back on what it needed to be. "Did your mother make good ones or hockey puck ones? My mother's were like neutron stars."

"My mom made stuff you'd find in the bottom of a coal mine. But the ones the lunch ladies made at the school cafeteria? Cheese biscuits, man. Flaky cheddar heaven." Yeah, okay, parking, parking. Fuck. He circled the block twice.

"Mmm... I like honey-buttered ones. Sugar on fat on sugar – drippy enough to have to eat with a fork."

"Uhn. Fuck, yeah." There. Artie hauled the Camaro into a spot about a block away from Greg and beat feet. He searched the streets for a white pick-up.

Greg was standing, carefully not touching anything, hands under his arms, just searching the street with huge, dark eyes. The man screamed "mug me." "You're close. The car just stopped."

Then the earpiece was pulled free, phone disconnected as Greg caught sight of him. "Hey. You found me."

"I did." He always seemed to. "So where are we heading to order supper?"

Greg looked pale but composed, dark circles under his eyes, his mouth a little tense. But considering the evening crowd?

Not bad.

"Oscar's. Soul food. Quiet. Take out." Greg found a smile for him, the look apologetic. "I didn't find what I was looking for."

"That's okay. Sometimes you do, sometimes you don't." The urge to touch Greg rode him hard, just to make sure...Fuck it. He let his fingers cup Greg's elbow. "You okay?"

He could feel Greg relax, lean into his hand. "Yes. I am. You didn't see his truck. and yes, I locked the doors before I left."

Lord. Sometimes he wondered what Greg would pick up from his head if they had sex. Not that he thought about it. Late at night with his hand on his dick and Duke locked in the bathroom. The

best way to deflate a stiffie was a Siamese cat
letting you know he'd seen better.

He steered Greg toward the green and yellow
neon sign that proclaimed their target food, just
shaking his head. The restaurant smelled good --
greasy and spicy and perfect. There were handfuls
of families, eating and laughing, kids giggling and
bouncing in the mismatched booths. Yeah. Perfect.

A round black lady grinned at them, grabbing
menus. "Y'all want to sit?"

Artie grabbed a menu from her, smiling right
back, working the charm a little. Go him. "Can we
order to go and sit and wait over here by the door?"

"Sure, honey. Just holler when you're ready."

Greg smiled, nodded at her, let him take both
menus. One episode in a restaurant was one too
many. That had been early on, before he'd
understood that Greg would let him push too hard,
let him push too far.

They ordered chicken and ribs and beans and
macaroni and biscuits and yeah, even greens.
They'd have leftovers tomorrow, which was good,
'cause he'd taken a day off. "Ooh, pecan pie."

"Oh, yum. There's milk at the house to wash it
down with, too." Greg stepped closer as a rugrat
barreled toward them, tripping on the loose rug.
Greg reached out, caught him instinctively, eyes
going wide a second. "Greens are not poison. He
was lying. They're good."

The kid looked up, mouth open. Then he ran off
hollering. "Moooommy!"

Artie cussed a little under his breath. "Sit, man.
I'll stand and run interference."

"I'm sorry." Greg swallowed hard, moving back
toward the chairs. He caught a glimpse as Greg

turned to look at the poster on the wall, hands buried in the dark jacket.

"Why?" Shit. He pushed Greg a little, right over where he wasn't touching anything but was out of the way. "You've had a rough couple of days."

"Yes, but ordering take out should not be a traumatic experience. You'd think I could manage it without scaring small children."

"Greg, man. You're not scaring him." More like freaking him out. "So. You wanna hear what Leah and I got?"

That got him a look, a nod, the kid forgotten, just like that. Damned bloodhound. "You know I do. Anything solid?"

"We've got six runaways that fit your profile. Blonde, young enough, yadda ya. Got uniforms doing door to doors." Beyond that? Bah humbug.

"Did you bring pictures? I didn't see much, but maybe I can help." Maybe. Of course, that was better than a lot of people could offer.

"I have the file in my car. When we get you home." When Greg was in a nice safe place, with his own shit around him. No way was he looking any sooner. "Man, that smells good, huh?"

"It does. Like Sunday supper. It was a good idea, detective. Food we can eat with our fingers." He got a full-blown smile, eyes just twinkling. "Duke's gonna be pissed at you."

"I'll take him a thigh. He loves thighs." Duke might forgive him if he did. And a little sliver of pecan pie. That cat had a fiendish sweet tooth. "Anyway, he's happy as long as I leave the remote on the coffee table."

Greg laughed, a real belly laugh that sort of filled up the place, Adam's apple just bobbing. "Game shows or infomercials?"

"Dog shows. On the animal channel. I think it makes him feel superior." That was much, much better. Artie touched, just a bit, his knuckles grazing Greg's hip.

"Oh, I can't blame him. It's not everyone that can say they own a detective." He needed to take Greg over to visit Duke soon. The fucking beast adored Greg with a singular passion. It was... obscene. Duke hadn't sat on anyone else's lap but Leah's husband's in five years. Maybe Duke was gay.

Their number came up, and Artie went and paid, grabbing three big bags of food. Hoo yeah. That smelled like heaven. "Thanks, honey. It's gonna make a couple of really happy men."

He turned. "You ready, Greg?"

The heavy duty growl of Greg's stomach answered him before Greg's nod did. "I am starving and ready to just dig in."

"Cool." It would take them about ten minutes now that he knew where the hell he was. The food would still be warm. "We got pie, so I'll go get doughnuts tomorrow, yeah?"

"And I'll make coffee." Greg nodded, walked with him, steady as you please. "The good stuff."

"Anything is better than station coffee." The unspoken "except yours" hung in the air as he walked Greg to the car, checking the street carefully, just in case.

"Oh, you haven't tasted Mitch's new non-caffeinated faux-coffee." Greg shuddered, face turning, looking, searching. "I think it's made from desiccated earthworms."

"There you go. That's gross." The Camaro looked fine, cherry-red and chrome shining in the streetlight, but he stopped Greg all the same and checked it over. Just in case. Then he opened the door, letting Greg brush against him a little. No one said he was a saint.

"Thank you. It is." Greg settled into the passenger's seat with a sigh, slipping on some thin gloves -- finger condoms he called them when things weren't serious. "I'll hold the food."

"Cool. Here goes." That holding food on his lap and driving thing? Not easy. They got out without anyone hitting them and headed for home...Greg's place.

"Don't touch the trash can." Greg walked well around it, balancing the food as those long legs took the back steps. The lid wasn't there, the top bag intact. Goddamnit. He'd bet his bottom dollar that son of a bitch had been here when Greg left. "Come on, Artie. Come in and eat. Don't forget the pictures."

"I got it." Grabbing the folder, he wandered in after, checking the danger spots. There was a shiny new lock on the back door. Thank God.

Greg handed him the food, unlocked the door. "I have new keys for you. Everything but the elevator. That's the same."

Just announce it out here in the open, professor. Christ.

"In, man. In." He wanted to get the fuck out of the alley. His neck itched. And he wanted ribs, too. With sauce. The kind you had to wear a bib to eat.

"Got it." There was nothing like the smell of Greg's apartment -- cinnamon and musk and eucalyptus and Greg. Damn. "Come on in. I'll get plates."

"Be right there." He dialed the precinct, got the drive-bys to come by more often, look for the white pickup. Then Artie got cups, silverware, leaving the folder in the kitchen when they headed out to sit at the table, not wanting it to ruin the meal. Oh, man. Biscuits. Damn.

Greg provided butter, honey, a bottle of hot sauce for the greens. Damn, it looked better than take-out, dished up and waiting on that shiny table.

Artie groaned, flopping down and digging in to fill his plate. "God, it's been a long week."

Greg nodded, stealing a biscuit first, slathering it with butter and honey. "The store had good sales this week, Alice said. People ramping up for Halloween. Lots of books on love spells and hexes and voodoo dolls."

"Lord, lord. It'll be crazy that night, huh?" All cops dreaded Halloween. "Agatha wanted me to take the kids trick-or-treating."

"You should bring them here. Alice has a whole thing planned -- kid-friendly and everything. They could rest in between hunting candy." Greg dug into the macaroni with a happy sound. "Alice and Mitch are dressing as Cupid and Psyche."

"That's...terrifying." Mitch as Cupid. Well, they always showed the little guy as kinda...doughy. "Do you really want the twins?"

"I'm staying in the office, but I'd like to see them." Greg shrugged, took some chicken, managing to lean over just in time not to drip on the pure white sweater. "I'll be near the elevator in case I get tired of the crush."

"It's a deal, then." His sister's kids were trying. But, hell, he and Agatha had been that way. "Jeez, that macaroni is to die for. Put that place on speed dial."

"The beans are up there, too. How're the greens?" Greg was leaning now, shoes off, relaxed. Better. Much better.

"Good. A judicious use of pork fat." Artie wiggled, settling his ass in his chair. Much, much better. Maybe they could have a slow couple of days.

Greg reached over, speared a bite from Artie's plate, and ate it. "Oh, not bad at all. I like."

Greg stole another bite, nodding.

He raised an eyebrow. "You got a thing against taking some for yourself?" Not that he minded, and Greg knew it. He just had to tease.

"Yes, detective. Yours tastes better." Greg grinned, stole another bite.

"Yeah? I wonder if your biscuit is better than mine..." He nabbed a bite, humming at the butter and honey taste.

"Well, of course it is! It's the perfect balance of butter and honey and bread." Greg looked almost affronted, except for the laughter in the dark eyes. "Now yours?" A chunk of biscuit was stolen. "Lacks enough butter. Too bready and cloying."

"Hey, it's a cholesterol bomb either way." He added some more hot sauce to the greens, just for Greg. "The ribs, though. They're perfect."

Feeling damned daring, he tore a bit of meat off and held it out.

"Perfect, huh?" He swallowed as Greg leaned over the waxed wood of the table, took the bite. Those lips brushed his fingertips as the pork was taken, and a soft breath that could have been a moan moved the tiny hairs on his fingers. "Oh."

"Mmmhmm. See?" Feeling a little breathless, Artie pulled his fingers back and licked them. "Good sauce."

Greg licked the sauce off his own lips, eyes focused and shining as that white sweater was pulled off. "Delicious. I didn't think I liked ribs."

"Yeah, well, you'd not had the right kind, then." Lord. Artie flushed. He'd always had thoughts like this about Greg, but he could usually control himself until he got home.

"Well, I haven't tried them in a long, long time. I'll know now."

Damn, he could almost see Greg's heart beating through the tight white T-shirt. He wondered what Greg could see through his baggy work pants. Right. Think about something else, Artie. "More chicken?"

"I..." Greg took a deep breath, blew it out and gave him a twisted little grin. "Yeah, a drumstick'll work."

Handing one over, he grinned back, just as wry. They had a lot to talk about. Damn it.

They got back to eating, laughing at the same old jokes, the same old shit. They were getting too damned good at this. Too good at hiding and pretending...what? That there was nothing there? "Man, I think it's time for pie."

"You want me to start the coffee?" Greg stood, passing close enough that Artie could smell him, smell his soap. "And do you want ice cream?"

"Yes and yes. And you touch that folder in there before dessert and I'll break your arm." The man didn't fool him one bit. Not one.

"Tsk, tsk. Police brutality, detective." Little shit.

"I'm off duty, bitch." The remains of supper needed to be packed up and put in the fridge. Artie got up to do it, wrapping up a thigh for Duke, snatching the folder and moving it before Greg could touch.

Greg just cackled, water from the coffeepot splashing on the counter. "Was that 'you're an off-duty bitch,' officer?"

"That, too. But ice cream and pie will sweeten me right up." Plates, pie, new forks.

The silver pie server was handed over, Greg doing the dishes quickly, easily. "Man, is that all you guys need? Good to know."

"Why do you think there're all the doughnut jokes?" He flopped pieces of pie over and turned to get the ice cream out of the freezer. And ran smack into Greg as he did the same thing.

"Oh!" Greg's eyes went huge, snapping to his as those long fingers wrapped around his upper arms.

"Sorry." They just stood there. He'd grabbed Greg's hips to keep him from falling and now he couldn't seem to let go.

"No, you're not." Greg blinked, flat belly moving against him. "I'm not either."

"No. I'm not." Thin pants. Greg had on those thin pants and that white T-shirt, and Artie's cock was just trying to open his zipper from the inside.

Greg closed his eyes, the want and need on the long, sharp-featured face sudden and harsh and real. "I know. I know."

"I...I don't know what to do about this, Greg."
He didn't. Artie stared right at Greg's Adam's
apple, not moving away. Swaying closer.

"I... What do you want?" Greg lifted his chin,
the hint of dark stubble right there, real as the heat
of Greg's prick against his hip.

"You." That throat was as irresistible as pecan
pie, so Artie leaned in and tasted it, lips open and
damp on Greg's skin. He'd worry about what might
happen if they got too intense later.

"Oh..." Greg swallowed, the soft moan just
vibrating under his lips. Those fingers slid, tracing
his arms, tickling his skin. Fascinating, the texture
there. Right at the hollow of the throat Greg's skin
went smooth, only the tiniest of fine lines marring
it. The bones there were sharp, the skin thin and
fine above them. So pointed, so sharp -- he could
tell from the hips in his hands, the bones pressing
against his palms.

Greg's ass wasn't sharp, though. It wasn't soft,
but it was round, the muscle hard where Artie slid
one hand back to grab it, rocking forward with his
own hips. God, his pants were scratchy. Maybe
Leah was right; he ought to buy some nice ones.

Greg chuckled, lips ghosting across his temple,
the kiss soft, the brief touch of Greg's tongue to his
skin intense as hell. "You're like a furnace. It's so
good."

"Yeah?" Well, he certainly felt like he was
burning up. Just standing there with Greg did more
for him than the last guy had with a full-on blow
job. "You're sharp."

Suave, Artie.

"Bony." Greg nodded, that stubble rasping his skin. Those hands slipped down, met on his belly and started moving again.

He sucked his gut in, his muscles going tight as he caught his breath. Oh, God. That felt... "Amazing."

"Yes. I've imagined, but the truth is better."

"Uh-huh. I thought about it a lot. I bet you know that." Well, of course Greg did. He didn't have to be psychic to know it.

"I do. I... I sit in your chair when you're gone, you know?" Oh. Oh, damn.

"I never knew that until the other day." Oh, hell. Just the thought made his cock jerk. Greg had to feel that. He nipped one sharp collarbone, resting his cheek on Greg's shoulder.

Greg moaned, one hand sliding up to brush his nipple, the other around his waist. "I don't know anything about seducing detectives, Artie."

"You don't have to. You're a natural." Finally he just did it, just went up on tiptoe and put his mouth against Greg's, sharing a kiss. Greg's eyes went wide for a second, then closed, tongue sliding and pushing into his lips, the kiss going deeper, the heat flaring. Fuck.
That wasn't just a flare of heat. It was like a solar explosion. His skin burned, and Artie started to pant, holding Greg in place to get more and more.

One hand cupped his head, long fingers cradling him. Greg stepped closer, held them both together. They leaned back against the counter, just tasting, learning what both of them had wondered about. Artie figured his legs would just melt soon.

"You. You are better than pie." Greg's eyes had green in them, tiny bursts of color he'd never seen before.

"Uh-huh. I need to sit down." Bad. Maybe in his chair.

"It's empty. Waiting for us." Greg nodded, moving them across the floor, refusing to let go. They stumbled against the coffee table, both of them grunting, but they made it, Artie falling back against the chair and pulling Greg down. Oh, hell yes. Pressure. Friction. Uhn.

Greg nodded, tilting his head up for another one of those kisses, Greg's lips pressing down against his, fingers framing his face. So fast. They'd just flashed so fast after all this time spent not touching and not looking and joking their way out of it. Artie arched up, his cock settling against Greg's pelvis.

"It's okay? Not too fast?" Greg licked his lips, panting into his mouth.

"No. It's good. Are you… You okay?" Tugging at Greg's T-shirt, he struggled to get it up and off, counting each rib, feeling the jutting angles of Greg's shoulder blades.

"Mmmhmm. Better than." Greg leaned back, stripped that shirt straight off. "You, too. Want to see you, too."

"Uhnkay." His shirt buttoned up the front, and, man, did that cause him trouble. Damn. The fucking thing was turning into a straightjacket. Greg chuckled, fingers fumbling with his, helping, leaning down to taste bits of his skin as it came into view.

"Oh." The touch of those lips just made his skin tingle. Like Greg was passing some kind of crazy energy into him through touch.

"Mmmhmm." Greg smiled, lips slip-sliding over his collarbone. He stroked Greg's back, scraped short nails over the vulnerable nape of Greg's neck. All he could reach with his mouth was Greg's ear, but that worked for nibbling. Greg arched, almost slipping off the chair, a surprised little gasp escaping him. "I... Oh. Sorry. It's been a while."

"'S'okay. I got it." Yanking Greg back, he kissed that mouth hard, loving the way that long, skinny body felt against him. Greg got settled against him, hips rolling a little, sliding the hard prick between them.

"Mmmm." Now if they could just line up. Like that. Shit, yeah. He didn't give a shit if he came in his too-rough pants. It was too good to stop and take any more off.

It didn't look like it was going to stop either, not the way Greg was bucking, riding against him like the man was starved for it.

"Greg. I need... oh, man. I think I'm gonna..." He lost it, eyes wide and kinda not seeing anything, his hips bucking like crazy.

"Artie!" Greg watched him, held him, hands splayed on his chest.

He panted. "Damn. Greg. Damn." Clumsy as they were, his hands moved, patting and petting. Greg just nodded, eyes huge, pupils dilated and focused on him. He reached between them, the heel of his hand pressing against the front of Greg's pants. "You, too, man. Definitely you."

Greg's head snapped back, throat working. Those pants were thin enough he could feel Greg's prick throb against his palm. God. Fucking hot. His own dick twitched a couple more times just watching, leaving him gasping. Moaning. And sweaty as hell.

"You... I... Wow." Greg leaned into him, heart just pounding against him. "Wow."

"Serious wow." The silence stretched between them after that, just sorta half comfy, half fragile, like they were afraid of what they might say. The touching didn't stop, though, random caresses happening over and over.

"Would you like some sweats? Something to wear for pie?" Greg was still touching, kissing, as if he couldn't stop, wouldn't stop.

"Uh-huh. And then. Uh. The ice cream is melting." It was sitting over there on the counter, no doubt ready to ooze off onto the floor. If they were at his place that would be okay, as Duke would play Hoover, but Greg liked the neat.

"Yeah. I have a mop." Greg's fingers found his nipple, tracing around it slowly.

"Oh. Okay. Well, we can always have the pie later. With some whipped cream." He wiggled, ass scraping the chair. He spread his legs again, trying to get the wet to settle.

"Come on. You can get comfortable." Greg stood, swaying a little, eyes just dragging over him.

"Comfy is good." The minute he got up he shucked the pants, amazingly not one bit self-conscious about his scarred-up thigh or his wet danglies.

Greg's fingers touched his thigh, wrapping around and holding it a minute. "I like it all."

"Yeah?" His cheeks flushed, a grin breaking out on his face. "Cool. I like your bony parts."

"You haven't seen them all." Greg headed over to the little partition separating the bedroom from the rest of the loft. "Yet."

Chapter Four

Artie was in his bed.

In his bed.

His bed.

Naked.

On purpose.

And no one had gotten there by accident or unconscious.

Greg poured another cup of coffee and blinked some more, heading back to sit next to Artie, close enough to touch.

In his bed.

Damn.

Artie rolled on his back, one arm whacking Greg's thigh and sitting heavily there. Artie was happy to be in his bed. Sated and happy and right at home. Dreaming about eating cheesecake. Off his belly. He hummed, one finger touching, tracing over muscles and planes. Artie was something else, something real. Something he had come to think of as home long before last night. That arm twitched, the heavy muscles pulling and moving. Artie was just wide everywhere, but not fat. Just heavy and solid and made to get the job done.

"Shh..." He kept petting, putting the coffee cup aside. He moved to that flat belly, the skin sprinkled with soft hair, so pale. Shiny. Artie looked fine on his white sheets.

"Mmmnnh." Artie moved again, but not restlessly. More like Duke when he was arching into a good scratching, all sinuous. Artie's belly rippled, every muscle moving as Artie's cock twitched and rose. Oh, now that was nice. He leaned down, cheek on Artie's belly, fingers trailing on Artie's hips.

"Greg?" Groggy, scratchy as a two-day beard, Artie's voice floated down to him, one big hand cupping his head.

"Last time I checked, yes." If more people could smell this -- the scent of Artie right here? There'd be less need for violence.

"Maybe I should check, man. Just to be sure. Do a little strip searching." Oh, damn. There was serious intent in that touch. Artie went from asleep to awake like *that*. He felt it through the rough skin of Artie's fingers.

So long. It had been so fucking long. "I can appreciate your attention to detail, detective."

"I like to make sure all of the bases are covered." Petting his hair, Artie chuckled, belly bouncing.

He grinned, turned his face to blow a raspberry on Artie's stomach, fingers sliding over to cup the heavy, soft balls.

"You're, oh. Pretty thorough yourself." Thighs spreading, Artie gave him more room, balls rolling against his palm. Damn, Artie liked that, liked the tiny hint of too much.

He kissed the tip of Artie's cock, then nipped the sensitive ridge, giving Artie a taste of his teeth, just a touch. "I've been thinking about this a long time. I can afford to be thorough."

"Uh-huh. I get that. Like it, too." Leaning up on one elbow, Artie started petting again, just stroking his neck and shoulders.

"You like touching." He rocked a little, cheek sliding down Artie's cock, then back up.

"I do. I like your skin. So smooth and pale." Artie liked his hair, too. And his eyes. He never knew Artie liked his eyes so much.

It made him burn inside, a steady flame that just wouldn't go away. "I watched you sleep; you didn't dream until the end."

He rolled Artie's balls, tongue dragging over the tip of the thick, heavy cock.

"I… Damn. I try not to." Thick and hot, Artie's cock dragged against his cheek, across his lips.

"I know." He loved the way the pale curls felt against his cheeks. "I know."

"Gonna come up here and kiss me?" Artie liked it, too. Maybe too much. That morning wood might pop, was what Artie was afraid of. It was cute as hell.

"Yes." He traveled back up, hands taking a slower, more convoluted trail. "Morning, Artie. You look good in my bed."

"Feels good here, man. Real good." Fingers sliding in his hair, Artie pulled him down and gave him a kiss, lips rubbing over his slowly, easily, before pushing in.

Oh. Oh, he'd forgotten. He'd forgotten how good it was. Greg settled against Artie, the shock of all their skin meeting together enough to make him shudder.

"Shhh. S'okay." So careful, so sweet. Artie could just go into protector mode so damned fast, fingers moving rhythmically on his back.

"It's so big. I just, I'd forgotten how to touch someone and it's you." He was babbling a little, but it was okay, it was Artie.

"Yeah. I kinda have, too, man. I just don't have your deal, you know? But it's been a long time and you. Well, you're it." Artie just looked him right in the eye.

"Yes." He just nodded; what else was there to say? This was Artie. "Yes."

He got a groan and another kiss, this one not careful at all. This one was hard and deep and so needy it ached. Their bodies slammed together, and Greg wasn't sure who was feeling what, who was moaning what words, and it didn't matter, not even a little bit. All that mattered was that they were touching and not waiting anymore. They toppled, Artie twisting so he was on the bottom, that heavy torso pressed against him. Artie kissed like he did everything, with a dogged determination that just never gave up. He wrapped one leg around Artie's hip, pushing up harder, demanding more. He got more; more kisses, more rubbing, Artie's cock against his hard and damp. That mouth. God. Artie had some serious talent.

"How... how come I didn't know you kissed like this?" He slid his hand down, thumb teasing a nipple briefly before continuing down.

"Because I don't know how I kiss?" Because most guys Artie had been with didn't like to kiss, thought it was girly and stupid. Artie liked it. A lot.

"Kissing is amazing. *Your* kisses are. Don't stop." He was a fan.

His fingers found that heavy cock and he groaned. Oh, he was a fan of that, too.

"Mmmhmm." Artie gave him everything. Lips swollen against his, Artie fucked his mouth and his hand, tongue pushing in as that cock rubbed and rubbed. And he got his quota of touching, too, every bump of his spine counted, the small of his back worshipped.

His toes curled. Fuck, he was aching, and he had to move, had to rub against that body and touch, and if he sort of shorted out, Artie'd have to forgive him.

"Greg." The rough way Artie said it told him loads about how far gone Artie was, too. So did the tension in Artie's body. Neither one of them was gonna last long.

"Yes. Yes. Please, Artie." He tugged a little harder, his own cock catching between them just right.

"Oh. Oh, fuck. God." That was it. Just like last night, Artie let loose, coming like a ton of bricks. It was a raw, pure feeling, just hot and wet and full of Artie's white noise as he shorted out.

He might have come, he might not -- he got caught in Artie's orgasm, entire body shaking with it and nothing else mattered.

They came down slowly, both panting and kind of shaking. Artie's eyes were almost black, the pupils still dilated, when they met his. "You're gonna ruin me, man."

"It's big. The... us." He rested his head on Artie's shoulder.

"It is. I knew it would be. Hey, we got leftover pie."

"Mmmhmm. Coffee, too."

There they went again. But maybe it wasn't such a bad idea to take this slow, talk about it in stages. Have pie.

They'd been waiting for years. A nice cup of coffee wouldn't hurt a thing.

Maybe they could go feed Duke.

***

Interesting.

He has always known Pearsall was a slut. The man had been before, flaunting himself with the little red-head artist, meeting in bars, dancing. Laughing like there was a joke no one else knew.

He watches the video flicker as another tape ends and he hits rewind.

Slut.

He takes his knife, wipes the blade clean. "Do you see? Do you see what happens when you sink into the filth? Do you see? He has been clean for so long and all it took was one touch."

The whimpers are softer now than they had been earlier this week, even an hour ago. So lovely. Just the barest repairs necessary. He drags the knife along his palm, the infected skin breaking open, pus pouring out. "You did. You little bitch. You bit me and you were dirty. Dirty just like all of them. Not worth collecting."

Not worth keeping.

Chapter Five

Duke was Not Pleased.

Why it was that the damned cat spoke in capital letters when he was pissed, Artie had no idea. But he did. The chicken thigh went a ways toward pacifying him. The Krispy Kreme cookies and cream doughnut helped. But it wasn't until Duke was firmly ensconced on Greg's lap, growling and hissing every time Artie came near, that the damned fiend seemed happy.

"Asshole cat."

"He's beautiful." Greg was crosslegged in the middle of Artie's bed, cradling and stroking Duke, long fingers smoothing the ruffled fur. "He missed you."

"Bullshit." Artie stretched, pulled his T-shirt off over his head, and tossed his pancake holster on the table. "Whassa matter, Duke? I didn't leave you enough credit on pay-per-view?"

Duke ruffled and hissed, Greg hushing him and stroking Duke's ears. Man, that move would get him torn to ribbons. "What kind of movies does Duke order? Porn?"

"He likes swashbucklers. The ones with the pretty boys. And girls." Artie tilted his head. "I think he's bi."

Greg laughed, "Sweet baby. He abuses you, doesn't he? No cream and tuna and long bouts of brushing?"

"The last time I tried to brush him for any longer than it took to get him smooth? He tried to eat my left nut. Don't let him fool you. You want more coffee?" Greg had made the coffee, because Lord knew he couldn't.

"Oh, no eating those, now, sweet boy. Those are too pretty to ruin." Greg nodded, held out the coffee cup with a smile.

He got it happily, knowing that the squalor would get to Greg eventually, but happy as hell that he looked so comfy right now. Just a different place could make some of the tension go away, sometimes.

Greg pulled some of his books down from the headboard and began organizing them, sorting them, eyes widening every so often, something slipping through those long fingers. "Oh, you liked the one about the Civil War."

"Yeah. It was full of neat stuff." Like how surgery was done on the battlefield, but no way was he gonna say that, what with the surgery book.

Greg nodded, put the books in order, settled in the middle of all the sheets looking just fine, just relaxed.

It made him smile. Made him brave Duke, bringing his own coffee over, and the extra doughnuts, and sit next to Greg on the bed. "Hey."

"Hey." Greg looked over, hand reaching out then brushing something off his bottom lip. "It's like the calm before the storm, isn't it?"

"It is, yeah." Greg tasted like latte and glaze and, well, Duke hair. Artie grinned. "But I've always been one to take the good where it comes."

"Yeah. The alternative sucks." Greg leaned in, licked the corner of his mouth. "You taste so good."

"Like sugar, huh?" His tongue pushed out, licking Greg's lips in return. "And you taste like coffee."

"Sugar goes in coffee just fine." Greg stopped, grinned at him. "Okay, that? Was lame. Funny and true, but lame. Remember I was a professor, not a lothario."

"Oh, I liked it, man." Not that he was picky. His idea of a pick-up line had always been, "You wanna?"

"I wanna." Duke hissed and jumped off Greg's lap as Greg pressed closer. "I mean, I'm glad you liked it."

"Wait." Archie got up and closed the bedroom door after Duke, the lock clicking into place. Then Artie did a cannonball, bouncing on the bed, rolling the mattress crazily.

Greg rolled into him, laughing hard, gasping when they came together.

"Mmm." That laugh made him happy deep in his belly. He'd bet Greg knew it, too, balls to bones. Oh. Balls. Artie thought maybe it was his turn to smell and taste and feel.

His neck got attacked, teeth and tongue making him shiver, but distracting Greg enough to get rid of the shirt, expose that whole long line of pale skin. Yeah. Oh, man. He scraped Greg's skin with his short nails, watching goose bumps rise. Then he pushed Greg on his back, nuzzling just under the right ear.

Greg moaned low, arching up under him. "Fuck, I feel you."

"You should. Want to taste you. Touch every bit." He'd waited too long. And as good as Greg had felt last night? Well, now they were in his bed.

Greg's hands splayed across his back, a deep sound pushing out of the long throat as Greg nodded. "Yes. Less clothes. More skin."

"Uh-huh." Pants. Shirt. Socks, because not sexy. They were naked in no time, and Artie celebrated it by sucking Greg's nipples, really giving them a go. "Taste so good."

"S...s...so good. Artie. Your mouth." He thought there ought to be a prize for getting a professor to babble.

"Greg." Artie just rubbed, rocked, nibbling, then biting. The little sounds got louder, deeper, each one asking him for more. Christ, how long had it been since anyone touched Greg, since Greg got to touch back? Too long, but he just couldn't complain. If he had to share Greg with Duke, so be it. But no one else. He slid down that flat, flat belly, following the trail to glory, just like that.

"Not letting that cat anywhere near my naked cock, Artie. Not a chance."

"He can sit on your lap. But that's it, man." There. The prize of prizes waited for him, and Artie licked at the head of Greg's cock, tasting the bitter salt and musk flavor. The sheets creaked, twisted in Greg's fingers, and God knew what Greg saw there, because that long cock throbbed and the clear drops started flowing faster, rising to meet his tongue. Sweet. Every one fell right on his tongue as Artie opened up and pushed down, taking Greg's cock down his throat as far as he could.

His name rang out, Greg's voice shocked, stunned, and surprisingly hot, all rough and raw like that. Those hips were pointed as a skinny nag's, the bones sharp as they moved under his hands.

So different from his own body. His own hips were just barely cut, his muscles standing out. He knew it from lying in this very bed and touching himself and wondering what Greg felt like. Now he knew, and it blew him away. Closing his lips hard around Greg, he pulled back, then slid down again.

"Thought about you. Dreamed. All around me, Artie. Sweet lord. All around me." Greg started moving in time with his lips, hips driving the rhythm a little faster, a little harder.

Artie just lost himself in it. What a fucking rush, having Greg in his mouth, calling his name, that hot skin all his to explore. Made him hard as a fucking diamond, made him want to just keep on forever.

"Forever. Your *mouth*, Art." Greg shifted, pushing against his hands, cock throbbing in his lips.

"Mmmhmm." He woulda grinned if he could have. Instead he cupped Greg's balls, just rolling them lightly, feeling the difference between that skin and the smooth, hot cock.

Oh, now. That got him a whimper, a desperate little shudder. Artie went down, opening his throat, and swallowed, silently begging Greg to come, to let him feel it. Taste it. Greg's cock jerked, bumping the back of his throat as heat sprayed, filling his mouth.

He moaned, working his tongue to help get it all, swallowing hard. Then he pulled back to kiss the head of Greg's prick. "God, that's good."

Greg nodded, blinking down at him, looking just stunned.

"You okay?" He was starting to worry a little the way Greg just lay there. Like maybe Artie had broken something.

"Yeah." Greg reached out, drew him up into a kiss, tongue pressing into his lips, tasting him. Oh, hell, yes. Artie just ate that kiss up like he would squash casserole at a church social. Damn.

Greg came alive underneath him, responding and repeating the touches, the motions that made him ache. His cock ached, and Artie just arched into the touch, body moving restlessly. He wanted...well. He wanted everything, didn't he?

"What do you want?" Those dark eyes held his, watched him, wanted him. "What do you need?"

"I need. I-- Touch me." His whole body shook, his cheeks so hot. God. Yeah.

Greg pushed at him, rolled him over, and straddled his hips, hands flat on his chest, fingers moving. "You're like a wet dream. My wet dream."

"Yeah?" That was just... Man. That was sexy as hell. He stared up at Greg, touching all over. The chest, the bony elbows, the belly. It was a feast.

"Yeah. I wondered, now I know." Every inch of him was explored, stroked. Greg whispered the name of each muscle as those long fingers touched it, the act so *Greg* that it made him smile. He was still smiling when Greg touched his cock. Then he started gasping, pushing, a lot closer to the edge than he thought.

"You're thick. You'll stretch me." Those fingers slid down his shaft, just barely brushing. "You are going to fuck me, aren't you? Let me feel you?"

"Now?" His voice squeaked. "I don't think I'll last, man. But soon? Yeah. Hoo yeah. So gonna."

"Not now." Greg chuckled, both hands wrapping around his cock and pumping. "Now I just want to watch you come, detective."

"Okay." Like Greg's voice was a trigger, Artie shot, just like that, hot and wet over Greg's hand. He flopped back on the bed and cracked the hell up when Duke's yowl outside the door echoed his own harsh cry.

Greg snorted, hands still wrapped around his prick as the soft laughter started.

"I think he's jealous." And it was a damned good thing he knew what Greg was laughing at, or his dick might just try to shrivel up.

"I know he is, and you have a fine fucking cock, Artie. Thick and hot. Longer than I imagined it."

"You're more substantial. Not your cock. Just the everything else." Greg was still too fucking skinny. But he was heavier than Artie'd thought.

He got a grin, Greg leaning down to kiss one nipple. "I'd forgotten about the afterglow part."

"Are you a snuggler?" Artie could be. He'd had one guy once who'd rolled off and gotten dressed and gone home, every time. That was lowering for sure.

"Really? I don't want to leave. I just want to feel you." That was unnerving as fuck, but the way Greg snuggled made up for it. He knew it. Knew it was the way it was when Greg touched things and all, and this close? Sharing this kind of connection, things would flow. It was cool. Greg hummed soft and low, the covers tugged over them. "We can rest a minute?"

"Uh-huh. We can hang out. Think about doing it again. Think about more food." He grinned, arm sliding to pull Greg closer, getting all the angles right.

"You're a bottomless pit." Right, like Greg could talk. "Duke gonna be okay?"

"Oh, he'll shred my sports coat. Then he'll watch a movie or something." His fingers kept coming back to one hipbone, tracing it over and over.

"That sports coat has seen better days." Greg just purred, cuddling into him with a sigh.

"Hey! I like it. It's comfy and it hides my gun." Just like his pillows were a little lumpy but shaped to him.

"I do like the way it makes your ass look." The compliment was just offered, casual and easy.

"Cool." Then it hit him what Greg'd said and he got tickled, chuckling like crazy. "You perv. You've been watching my ass all this time."

"Artie. Any gay man with eyes and the sense God gave a goat watches your ass."

He flushed hot. "Leah says some of the girls do, too. You, though? I like." Like was such a weak word for it.

"Yeah. You're good for me. Good to me." Greg kissed his chest. "And those girls don't know what they're missing."

"This is true. They'd never make it past Duke."

Chapter Six

The chrysanthemums were beautiful, blooms big as saucers, almost drooping on their stems. Orange, white, rust, even one variegated series -- Doctor Van Hoord would be proud of him. Greg could remember her, tiny and wizened and odd, snapping out information on genus and phyla, her graduate students panicked and scribbling.

He moved the little wheelbarrow to the heirloom roses, pruning them back almost viciously. Such a violent act, pruning. Snipping off healthy branches for the well-being of the plant. Shears snipping and snapping and cutting deep, sap wetting the blades like blood or tears or...

"Oh, for Chrissake, Gregory, get a fucking grip. It's *gardening*." The sound of his own voice, irritated and clipped, made him chuckle, got him back on track. Sometimes things just needed to be about dirt and worms and manure or a man might lose his mind.

"Should I get near you with those clippers in your hand?"

He jumped, clippers clattering to the rooftop. "Shit! You scared me. Damn. Hey. Hi. Sorry, I was in the zone."

"I tried to call your cell. You should carry it with you, Greg. Just in case." Artie looked, if anything, even more tired. Damn.

"I have it up here. Somewhere." Turned off. He thought. Maybe. He found Artie a smile. "You want a coffee?"

"Yeah. That sounds good. Are you done? I don't want to interrupt the communing."

"Less communing, more pruning." He wheeled the rose branches to the compost heap, tossing them in with the rest.

"Then coffee sounds good. It really does." Scrubbing a hand over his face, Artie waited for him to lead the way, shoulders slumping a little. Okay, a lot.

"You off duty, detective?" If so, Greg was so dumping Artie into the tub with some lavender oil and a little Bach. The man needed a break.

"I am. I tell you, man, folks have gone crazy. It must be the season, or something. We got two more cases dumped on us today, and Leah is all swollen." Artie leaned against the roof unit while he put shit away and opened the door.

"I'll have Alice call her. There are things that help." He got everything locked away, ignoring the tiny little flashes that told him Alice had been here to water and some teenagers hade come hoping for marijuana. "Come downstairs. I'll run you a bath."

"Yeah?" Those eyes lit up, Artie reaching out to touch him, just barely grazing his shoulder. "That would be great."

"Your hands are always warm."

They headed down the stairs, the old wood creaking under their feet.

"Obviously I'm just a hot guy." There it was --
that hint of humor, the ghost of a smile in Artie's
voice. Better.

"Most definitely. Still, I think a long soak and a
backrub..." Oh. He could give Artie a backrub.
This whole touching thing was getting better and
better.

They reached the landing and Artie grabbed
him, hauling him around for a kiss. Looked like
someone else liked that idea. A lot.

His eyes felt huge, hands cupping Artie's face.
The heat, the flood of want, felt good.

Solid and hot against him, Artie held him close,
lips moving over his. He could feel how much
Artie had wanted to call him when Leah had to go
home early, could feel how bad Artie had felt for
the mom of the little girl who'd gotten hit by a car.

"Anytime. I'll leave it on. You call." He pushed
back into the kisses, trying to rub the aches and
hurts away.

"You're good to me, man. Anything...well.
Anything in the mail?" The question hung there,
reluctant, waiting.

"I didn't go downstairs." He wanted be alive.
Awake. Just himself.

"Alice knows to tell you, though, right? I don't
want another phone call like the last one. You were
messed up." It wasn't the cop talking. It was his
newfound lover. It was at once odd and
comforting.

"She does. No more phone calls. Come take a
bath with me. I'll touch you."

"Okay." Following along, hands skating over
his clothes, his exposed skin, Artie came with him,

hungry as anything. Just needing so badly you didn't have to be psychic to see it.

They went inside his flat, leaving the coffee and heading straight back for the big bathroom with the garden tub. The oils. The gardenias in the windows. The fuzzy towels. "Get naked. You like the water hot."

"I do. And I like the smell of that stuff you use." Shoes, pants, shirt, Artie stripped for him, not a bit self conscious.

He got the water started, poured the oils in. "Turn on the stereo and I'll put towels on the radiator stand."

He was almost vibrating, so excited, so thrilled to have this, to do this.

"Anything you want in particular?" Like Artie would put anything on but mellow jazz. When the music was floating around them, Artie came back and looped strong arms around him, lips on his neck.

He leaned his head forward, unbuttoning his shirt while offering Artie more of his nape, more of his skin.

"Mmmm. Oh, that's a cure for what ails me. For sure." Those lips moved, tickling the tiny hairs on the base of his neck, sliding across to sit under his ear, smooth and damp and warm. The sound he made was a little desperate, a little needy, a lot wanting, and it was no surprise that his cock pushed right on out when he popped the button on his fly.

"Oh. Damn, Greg. You smell good." Artie was hard, too, pressing against his ass, one hand dropping to cup his cock, fingers pressing the head. "Feels so soft. Your skin, I mean. The rest is hard."

"Your hands." He got the rest of his clothes off, leaned back all the way into those arms. "God, Artie."

"No one has ever even mentioned my hands before, man." If he opened his eyes and looked down at Artie's hands on him, he couldn't see the brief flashes of nameless faces that had come in and out of Artie's life so fast. So fast. No one had ever *gotten* Artie before.

"No one looked. Come in the water." His fingers slid over the top of Artie's, tracing each line, each knuckle, every inch.

"Mmmhmm. As soon as I can move. You're killing me, man." They swayed, Artie's solid body just pushing and pressing.

"No. Loving you. You like it." He drew their hands down, slid them over his hips.

"I do." Rough fingers rubbed over his hipbones, under them, forefingers pressing along the seam of his torso and thigh.

His breath caught, eyes closing, heat rushing through him. "Please don't stop."

"Not gonna. Though it'd be a shame to waste that hot water. Come on. Get in." Muscling him like he weighed nothing, even though he was half a head taller, Artie moved them to the tub, getting them all settled inside, arms and legs tangled.

Greg leaned back, stretching out against Artie with a soft sigh. "You good?"

"I am so good you don't even know." He got a warm, damp chuckle. "Or maybe you do."

That tickled him, got him to laughing, soft and deep. "There is very little that hot water and naked skin can't fix."

"You got that right. You've got this spot, right here..." Oh. Oh, God, when Artie touched the underside of his thigh like that, Greg saw fireworks. His toes curled and he rippled, his gasp just echoing and echoing.

"And... and you have one on your wrist. Here." Greg's fingertips found it, drew a slow lazy circle around it.

Artie's cock jerked against Greg's back. "I do. Oh, damn, Greg. That's good."

He nodded, drew that hand up to his mouth, lips and teeth working that little sweet spot. Yeah. Yeah, it was good.

Grunting, moving hard enough to make the water slosh, Artie rubbed, practically purring. That rough, half-broken voice just went right through him, making him shiver. The shaking intensified when Artie used his free hand to touch and stroke, reaching down to cup Greg's cock again.

Hard enough he ached, Greg just whimpered, hips rocking, floating in the water and trying to push toward that hand. "I feel you. Lord. It's... It's fine, Artie."

"Uh-huh. Good. I...smells good. Feels right." They rocked, Artie pressing up against him, fingers closing around him nice and firm, pulling.

He nodded, stubble making a rough noise against Artie's inner arm. Every place that flushed on that muscled arm he nuzzled and nipped, leaving his mark. Groaning, panting, Artie just let him go, watching him, kissing his shoulders. The fascination hadn't faded at all with a little familiarity. In fact, Artie seemed even more intent on him.

He licked the light band of skin Artie's grandpa-watch usually covered, the curve of elbow that smelled warm and musky, the puckered bit of skin from a fight back when Artie was a rookie and working the streets.

All the while Artie worked him, too, hand moving on him, from tip to base and below to tease his balls, then back up. When Artie started getting toothy he knew the impatience was building. The need. He shifted his hips back, Artie's heavy cock sliding along his crease. He smiled as Artie groaned, bucked a little. Oh, someone liked that.

So he did it again.

"God. Greg. That. Damn." Growly. That rough-as-gravel voice just scraped over his nerves.

"Yeah." He was almost humming with it, lifting himself up a little in the water and then easing himself back down, rubbing that sensitive shaft the whole way.

The hand around him tightened, using his cock as leverage to pull him back even harder. They became a circle of pleasure, from Artie's hand on him to his ass rubbing that thick prick. It was -- oh, sweet fuck. With the water splashing against him and his nipples hard and that hand and Artie's need all mingled with his and... "Artie. Artie, I. You."

"Got me, Greg. Any way you want me. Not gonna hurt you, though." No. No, Artie wouldn't ever do that. He hated it when anyone did with a passion that burned almost as bright as Artie's want.

"No. No, you won't. I know. Please." Come to bed, Artie. Come to bed.

"Yeah. Yeah, okay." Artie grunted, legs and arms and belly muscles going tense as Artie heaved them up out of the tub, water just streaming everywhere. God, that man had brute strength.

Greg moaned, grabbing a towel as soon as Artie let his feet hit the floor, getting the bare minimum of water off them before heading for the bed.

Following close on his heels, Artie pushed him down on the bed and reached unerringly for the lube in the side table, settling between his spread legs. "Fuck, Greg. Pretty."

He drew his legs up and back, spreading wider, trying not to feel like he hadn't been a lot younger last time he'd done this.

"Gonna be good, Greg. Gonna be fine." Bless him, Artie knew. Knew and took such care, getting his fingers good and wet before pressing them between Greg's legs, right up against his hole. The other big hand stroked his belly, soothing him.

He moaned, arching a little under the touch. "Your hands..."

Artie wanted to say they were made for touching him but thought it was too corny. Too cute. One finger circled his hole, pushing and pressing. Opening him up, Artie pushed in deeper, all the way in, finger crooking inside him.

He cried out, the jolt inside of him strong, almost shocking. "Oh. Again. Not hurting me. Please. Do it again."

"You got it." He did, too, Artie teasing him, testing him, finger sliding in and out. When he became slick, open and easy, a second finger joined the first, pushing him higher and higher.

It was amazing, the way things felt, the way Artie pushed inside him. Greg kept his eyes open, kept watching, assuring himself he was there. Real. Solid.

"Right here. God, you're hot inside." Hot, and tight, and Artie could hardly believe it either. Greg felt the awe. "One more, man? I don't want to push too hard."

"I stretch." He reached out, eyes wide as his hand landed on Artie's chest. The strong heart beat and beat, so steady. "One more."

"One more," Artie repeated, licking his lips and nodding. The hand not partly inside him moved, fingers searching out the sweet spot on his thigh as Artie pushed that third finger inside him, so good.

"Artie." A soft sound pushed out of him and he wanted, he wanted it all, so badly he ached. "Please."

"Now, huh? Yeah. Now." Artie pulled free and got the lube again, slicking up that cock, all red and hard for him, so hot. So hot. When Artie pushed against him with the wet head, he thought he might explode.

Damn. Oh, damn. Exploding might be smaller than this, might be less than the feeling of Artie inside him.

Pushing forward, Artie stretched him to the breaking point, thick and so hard, all the way in until Artie's hips cupped his ass. He moaned, eyes clinging to Artie's. Inside him. Christ. It took all he was to remember to breathe in, to suck in air. A deep, rough sound rumbled up from Artie's chest, hips surging as he started to rock against Greg, filling him over and over. Tremors began deep inside Greg, threatening to shake him apart, to take him apart. Then Artie's hand landed on his belly, easing him, centering him right down.

"I got you. I'm right here, Greg. I'm with you all the way." Sweet touches soothed him, calmed him enough to breathe and relax, letting Artie in even deeper.

"Oh..." He rippled, the smile stretching his face. "Yes. I know. I *know*, Artie."

He got a smile in return, Artie rocking into him, hands starting to move on his skin. His throat, his chest, his upper arms all felt Artie's touch before those rough fingers found his nipples and pinched. That brought out more of those hungry cries, and he lifted up, tugging Artie down for a kiss. The kiss turned voracious right off, Artie licking at his lips, invading his mouth with that hot tongue. He groaned, wrapping his lips around Artie's tongue and sucking. His cock rubbed between them, caught against Artie's heat.

"Mmm." The man sounded like Greg was cheesecake. Or hot chocolate. Artie loved hot chocolate with real milk and marshmallows. He almost laughed as that popped into his head, but then Artie moved just so, hit that spot inside him the very best way.

He gasped, nodded. Oh. Oh, yes. Love. There. Good. Don't stop. Somehow, Artie heard, knew, he could feel it. It just kept on and on, Artie's face and chest flushed dark, the arm muscles with the marks Greg'd left standing out strong as Artie grasped his hips.

"Soon. Soon, Artie. I'm going to shake apart." Either that or die. Or come. Something.

"I can't hold it, man. Can't." He could see it in those cloudy eyes, could feel it in Artie's touch as that hand wrapped around his cock, pulling hard.

He felt it, that unbelievable sink-ache-pull-fall deep inside him, and then it was too big to hold, and it poured from him, entire body jerking and clenching.

"Oh. Oh, fuck!" That was it. Artie came, too, shooting deep inside him, panting and wheezing.

That forced his eyes closed, a rush of *Artie* pouring through him, filling him.

Better. So much better. That was what passed from Artie's skin to him as they settled together, Artie flopping on him, surprising a grunt out of him.

He nodded, holding on. They could eat and drink coffee and talk later. Right now, this was enough, this was good.

***

His rumbling stomach woke him, and Artie stared up at the cloud-painted ceiling, wondered idly how long it had been since he ate. Greg felt too good to move, though, so Artie cuddled up.

Goddamn, it had been a frickin' rough day. Between all the shit he'd taken over Greg's case, from the secretary to the captain, and then him and Leah getting slapped with two new cases...well, it was a good thing Greg was warm and happy and easy to be with.

It still fucking amazed him. Just flat out sent him into orbit. He ran one hand down Greg's side, over ribs and hip to the long thigh.

Greg hummed, eyes moving quickly as Greg dreamed, a little smile on those lips.

He grinned, getting up on one elbow and looking down. Long, sharp angles, smooth, smooth skin. Pretty pretty. Like Greg could hear him, that long cock started to fill, to curve above the flat belly.

"Mmm." He hummed, too, his hand slipping up and around as Greg's legs fell open, cupping those balls. Sweet and fuzzy, they weighed heavy in his hand.

"Your hands." Greg's eyes fluttered, a soft laugh escaping. "I'm not fuzzy, am I?"

"Just right here. It's a good thing." Stroking those soft hairs, Artie moved up to the curls crowning Greg's growing cock. "I love how you feel."

Greg stretched out, "I used to ache for this. I'd sit in your chair and think."

"I'm still not sure how I got so lucky, man." It just floored him. Absolutely fucking killed him.

"It was that first phone call, when you called me a fucking lunatic and threatened to have me arrested. I was hooked."

Hooting, he smacked Greg's ass lightly. "So romantic. Amazing how you saw through me."

"Hey! I'm psychic!" Greg chuckled, sat up and kissed him, tongue sliding over his bottom lip.

"Mmmhmm. So what am I thinking now?"

"You're trying to decide whether we should eat now and go for two orgasms later or split them up and order in from Tuscana's."

His stomach grumbled again, and he laughed his ass off. "I think food, man. I'm starving."

Greg grinned, goosed him and nodded. "I have stew. Eggs. Uh... Fried rice."

"How about eggs and bacon and all to go with the coffee you promised me." Seemed like breakfast time. Even if it was only ten P.M.

"Now, why would a macrobiotic, clean-living, new-age store owner have bacon in his house?" Those eyes went wide and guileless. Bastard. The man loved anything greasy and bad for him.

"I know where you hide that little freezer. Alice may not. But I do." Yeah. Like Greg was an innocent. He snorted silently.

Greg grabbed a pair of sweats, tossed another pair toward him. "I don't see how she can think bacon is bad for you. It's like crispy heaven."

"It is, indeed. Lord knows, she just can't hack eating Wilbur or Charlotte or whatever." The sweats slid on easy, old and smooth and Greg's. Sexy.

"Charlotte was the spider. I've eaten spider, you know? In Colombia. It was... crunchy." Greg gave him a wink, eyes twinkling.

"That's gross, babe." He grinned. "Now spider crab? Deep fry it. Hoo yeah."

"Maja squinado?" Greg nodded. "Did you know that they migrate seasonally? It's quite fascinating, really..."

Christ, the man was near impossible to gross out.

"Nutbag." Scratching, Artie wandered toward the kitchen, somehow not grossed out enough to not be hungry. "I just like them in sushi. It's better if I don't know their personal habits."

Some nice thick bacon came out, along with frozen biscuits and a can of grape juice concentrate. "Now there's something we've never had together."

"Sushi? Can you handle that? All of that cutting and arranging and shit?" He thought about it a minute. "I bet Alice knows how to roll it, huh?"

"I don't know. I'll ask. Maybe I can learn. I used to love tuna nigiri."

Hell, to smooth away that wistful look? Artie might learn himself. Surely he could at least get the crab salad thingee right. Though the rice might be beyond him. He got out a frying pan for the bacon. He could do that, nice and crisp. Greg had to make the eggs all fluffy though.

"Is it rude to ask what you miss most?"

"Up until very recently? Sleeping next to someone." Greg handed him the bacon. "Now I miss going to the movies. Real popcorn. Huge image. The whole thing. I loved going before the accident."

"Yeah. Yeah, that would suck." He'd been able to lose himself in movies ever since he was a kid, when the sci-fi flicks started coming out, and the special effects were just awful. He bumped hips with Greg as they got the stove set up, just grinning.

"I manage okay. DVDs have special features." Greg kissed his cheek before heading for the eggs. "What's your favorite movie?"

"Promise not to laugh?" The bacon sizzled merrily away, waiting for him to flip it. One more second, yeah, that would get all of the bendy out of it. "*Raiders of the Lost Ark.*"

"Yeah? I love when the guys melt at the end. Too gory. Very cool. *Pulp Fiction* was the last movie I saw at the theater." Greg started whisking the eggs, whistling away.

"Man, I hated that movie." One, two, five. He was damned hungry. "It just made no sense, man."

"I went with a bunch of kids from my lab. I thought Sam Jackson was fascinating, but the violence factor? Eh."

"It was the constant cussing, man. It just made me deaf five minutes into the movie." Fuck, he could curse a blue streak if his momma wasn't around, but that? Had been excessive.

"Well, I imagine it's sort of antithetical to what you are, what you do for a living, Artie."

"A little, yeah." He went to feed Duke a piece of bacon before remembering where he was. That piece stopped just short of the floor, his hand cupping it.

Greg chuckled, applauded. "Poor Duke. I bet he misses you."

"Oh, he's living it up on the caviar he found under the counter, I bet." From Leah's last big thing with her hubby; she'd sent it home with him just for Duke. Artie played hide and seek with it weekly.

"Oh, you should get him a fish tank. He'd watch it for hours." The biscuits beeped in the microwave and the eggs got dumped in a bowl.

"He would. But then he'd *eat* them. Did I ever tell you that Leah had a lizard once?" Man, she'd babysat Duke. There had been monitor parts all over the place. Ick.

"Uh-oh." Greg's nose wrinkled. "How long did it take to clean it up?"

"Oh, not long. It was the endless 'your cat ate my pet' harangue that took forever." Artie shuddered.

"Oh, lord." Greg looked at him. "Never let Duke near the baby."

Hooting, he put the last of the bacon on a paper towel lined plate. "You should see him, Greg.

Curling up next to Leah's belly and *talking* to the sprog."

"Yeah? No shit? You'll have to take a picture. I want to see." They got the mess of food to the table, Greg grabbing the honey and butter and hot sauce on the way.

"He's fucking hilarious. He wants it out now so they can commune." That silly cat was in love. Big time. Not as much as he was with Greg. But close.

"Poor Leah. Maybe she's got a built-in babysitter with him."

"Maybe. Though her hubster would be terrified." Yeah, well. It wasn't his fault they didn't get along. Duke was just...picky. And possessive. And, uh. Crazy. He forked up some eggs right out of the bowl. "Mmm."

"Enough salt?" Greg was pottering again, plates and napkins, coffee and juice and milk, this and that.

"Uh-huh. Come eat, man. You're skin and bones." Waggling his eyebrow, Artie teased, "Though I like jumping your bones."

"What are your thoughts about my skin?" Greg sat next to him, fingers sliding along his thigh.

"It's soft." Soft and smooth, except where it wasn't, the little patches of fuzzy that Greg didn't like to admit were there, so damned intriguing.

"Oh." He got another grin, then Greg reached for a biscuit. "I don't have any blackberry jam, will honey work?"

"Yeah. It will work just fine." His cock jolted, honey and Greg's skin and the brush of that arm across his chest conspiring to make him gasp.

The biscuit fell to the table, Greg's eyes wide. "Oh, we'll never finish eating if you think things like that."

Throat tight, Artie nodded, picking up the biscuit and feeding Greg a bite with honey on it. "I know. I just. Damn."

Greg nodded, licking his fingers clean with a soft, hot tongue, catching the drips of honey. Uhn. Artie shuddered, thinking a whole lot more of those kinds of thoughts. The ones that made Greg start to pant as Artie thought them.

"Eat your eggs, Artie." Greg's mouth found the pulse point on his wrist, eyes closing.

"Bacon..." They'd have to eat the bacon. It sucked warmed over.

"Uh-huh. No limpness. Limposity. Limpitude."

"Right." Limp? Nope. Not a bit. He leaned in and licked a drop of honey off Greg's lips.

Fuck, that husky little sound was worth writing home about. "We were going to eat first."

Greg shifted, picked up another bite of biscuit and fed it to him.

"We were. Are." Hell, he really couldn't do it again without food. They made their way through the whole meal by eating off each others' fingers. Hot and sensual and surprisingly relaxing, they managed to eat it all without jumping each other's bones.

Artie blinked when all of the food was gone. "Hey. We ate."

"We did. What good people we are, not wasting food."

"Starving children in Africa and all." Witty. Lovely. Artie just leaned, moving up against Greg.

"Mmmhmm." Greg settled in his lap, eyelids fluttering for just a second. "Do you know how many pieces of furniture I haven't seduced someone on in here?"

"I bet I do. There's like, my chair and your bed that you have. Where next?" Here seemed good. Excellent in fact.

"Yeah. I like here. The bathtub's been used. We'll have to try the cabinet sometime." Those long fingers framed his face.

Just the thought of that made him overheat like a toaster with a bagel stuck in it. Artie chuckled. What a thought. "That sounds like a plan, you know?"

"Yeah. Yeah, I know." Greg chuckled, leaning in to kiss him, tongue pushing right in to taste him.

"Mmm." All he could do was hum and clutch Greg to him and kiss back. He explored and tasted, pushing the kiss deeper and harder.

Greg moaned into him, hips rocking, rubbing against Artie's belly and making all sorts of promises.

"Love the way you...Greg. Damn." He loved it all, so how was he supposed to pick one thing? He touched, that fine, fine skin sliding under his fingers, the tiniest bit of honey making them catch here and there.

Greg nodded, nibbling on his lips, eyes staring into his like he was fascinating.

"Greg. Want you." His damned libido went into overdrive these days, now that he was able to touch, to see and smell and… Yeah. Artie kissed Greg until that long body bent back over his arm, shoulders nearly touching his legs.

"Don't let me fall." Greg stretched, that trust heady, intense.

Fuck, he could feel those angles, those lean muscles, all just given up.

"Not gonna." No way. Not ever. Well, not if he had any say. He couldn't protect Greg when he wasn't there. Now he could, though, and he supported Greg's back, licking and kissing that long throat.

"God, Artie. That feels..." He heard Greg's moan, felt Greg swallow. "It's like the first time all over. So good."

"You're amazing, babe." Babbling. That was what he was doing. Just telling Greg all sorts of shit, with his words and his hands. All about how he'd wanted and needed and finally gotten and now couldn't get enough. Reaching inside Greg's sweats with his free hand, Artie touched the long cock, fingers pressing the sensitive spots.

"Oh. Oh. Shouldn't have made you wait so long. I was scared. Scared I'd short out on you."

"I know. And I was so scared I'd hurt you. Fuck with your head." Hot. Hot and beating with Greg's heart, that cock filled his hand and then some. Jesus.

"Never hurt me. You don't. Artie, I feel you. Good." Greg was moaning, flushed, rocking into his touch.

Losing the ability to do anything but nod, he groaned and stroked, watching Greg swell harder, watching that fine body writhe and buck. He could see the orgasm pass through Greg -- the long belly flushed dark, balls drew up, cock jerked as Greg's cry just echoed and heat sprayed, pooling on Greg's belly.

"Oh. Oh, fuck, man. I can't. Jeez." Greg hadn't even touched him, his sweats still covered him, but Artie came anyway, like a house afire.

Greg shuddered. "Oh, shit. That's so sexy."

"Greg. Damn. We can add the kitchen table to the list." Well, the chair. The table had possibilities. "And there's my place, too."

"Mmm. Yeah. Your tub. Your sofa. The walls..."

"Walls." His back might never be the same. Back. Lord. Hauling Greg up, Artie kissed Greg's mouth soft and slow, stroking the strained spine.

"Oh." Greg melted against him, breathing nice and slow. "Your hands."

"You haven't even seen yet what I can do with them." Greg made him feel tall as a mountain and just as strong. "Want you to, though."

"Good. We have time. Time to learn." His shoulder was kissed, his collarbone.

"We do." All the time in the world. He'd see to it.

One way or the other.

Chapter Seven

Greg stared at the package.

At the wall.

At the package again.

Okay, there was no guarantee it was a package from him. Not at all.

Just because there wasn't a return address.

Or a label.

And the handwriting was the same.

And it made him sick just looking at it, and even Alice avoided touching it, and it was book shaped and he hadn't put in any little book orders.

What could that possibly mean?

The shop bell jingled, making him start, the low murmur of Alice's voice like the buzzing of a bee. Indistinct. The yowling of a Siamese cat came a lot clearer.

Artie appeared in the doorway to his little office, carrying a huge plastic carrier with a very unhappy Duke in it. "Hey, man. Alice called. I hope that's okay."

"Oh, Duke. You're ruffled." He nodded, looking up at Artie. "Is it that bad? That she knew to call?"

"Well, I imagine it ain't good. We were on the way back from the vet. Duke ate some tin foil. Can I close the door here and let him out? He'll calm right down if he can squat on you."

"Is he okay?" He nodded, reaching to open the cage, Duke yowling and spitting and pissed. "C'mere you. Poor thing."

"Well, he's just had like half a tuna can pulled out of his butt. But yeah." Poor Artie just gave Duke that hapless pet owner look, and Duke hopped right up on Greg's lap, telling him all about it. Loudly.

He nodded, stroking Duke's ears and listening, murmuring right back about how awful and smelly the damned vets were and how, maybe, tin foil was hard on the G.I. tract.

"He wanted that burrito, man. He even got the damned fridge open and levitated to the second shelf. So where's the mystery package?" His eyes cut right to it and Artie glanced over, lips tightening. "Same deal, huh?"

"Uh-huh." Greg looked at it, sighed, feeling two parts sick and three parts ashamed. "It came an hour ago."

"Okay. It's okay." Duke grumbled and settled, making a that's that sort of noise. Artie walked over to the package, pulling out a pen and poking at the wrapper. "No blood on the outside."

"No. It's a book. It looks like a book." He reached out, almost touched it, then pulled back a little. "I should open it, huh?"

"Yeah." A ferocious frown twisted Artie's face. "I don't want you to. But he does. And I'm worried what he'll escalate to if you don't."

"Okay. Okay." He reached out, grabbed the book with both hands and started unwrapping the butcher paper. Butcher paper, not regular paper. Butcher. By the time his fingers got to the book, sticky slick with blood, he was falling.

Dark. Still. Fuck, it was dark and wet, so wet it hurt to breathe. He shook his head, trying to get away from the smell.

"Greg! Shit. Come on, Greg. Let it go. Let go of the... come on." Artie was gagging, pulling at his hands, prying his fingers open.

No. No. He could almost see. Almost. Red lights. Red lights.

"I swear to God, if you puke on the evidence I'll set Duke loose in your kitchen. Babe. Please." He was retching, too, dry heaves, his whole body shaking. Artie finally pried his grip loose, the whole mess plopping on the floor with a horrible wet sound.

"Oh, God. Oh. Out. Out." He stood up and ran for the elevator, slamming his hand against the call button over and over. Water. He needed a shower. A bath. Bleach. Air. Light. Something.

"Stop." Arms going around him, Artie practically tackled him, holding him so he could barely move. Fuck. Strong. "Stop touching things. You'll just spread it all over and then what the fuck will you do? We'll get it off. We'll get you clean."

It was the rough edge of panic in Artie's voice as much as anything that stilled him. Artie never panicked.

"Please." He closed his eyes, started reciting the peripheral nerves, proximal to distal. "Spinal accessory, levator scapulae, thoracic, dorsal scapular, subclavian, suprascapular..."

The elevator came down and Artie hauled him in, Duke's sleek body slipping in between his feet. His stomach turned as they went up, but soon enough he stood at his sink, the water running warm and cleansing over his hands. Washing it all away.

"Artie. He's got another one. He's got another one in the dark. What *was* that?"

"I don't know. I need to go back down there and secure it, see what all it is. I. Babe." Artie had let him go and he stood there scrubbing, his skin getting raw. "I don't want to leave you alone, but I have to. Can you? Will you be all right? With Duke? Just for maybe a half hour. I swear."

"Go. I'm okay. I'm fine." Greg almost laughed, almost, because if he started, he'd never stop. He'd just laugh and laugh until he couldn't remember anything.

"Look at me." Those gray eyes held his when he turned, boring in. "I'll be right back. Go sit down. Let Duke tell you about the burrito. I'll be right back."

"Okay. Don't let Alice in there. She'll be pissed."

"No kidding. Sit. Breathe."

Then Artie left him, and the only thing left was the whooshing of the water and the sound of Duke purring as the silly cat rubbed around his ankles. He let himself sink to the floor, cheek against the sink, listening to the water run. "Oh, fuck. Duke. Guys like us weren't meant for shit like that."

Duke pushed against his belly, marking him, whiskers tickling through his shirt in a feline "no shit."

***

Bile rose in Artie's throat.

It was a kidney. Perfectly removed, excellently wrapped. The box around it had been shaped like a large book, hand cut to really give the look. The butcher paper could have come from anywhere, and goddamn it, there wasn't a fucking thing to go on.

"Yeah. Yeah, okay, thanks."

Leah flipped her cell closed. She looked greener around the gills than he felt. Bless her, she came though. "Dave says he'll run the blood and all tonight. The paper isn't likely to yield anything, and neither is the box. The handwriting is the same. You should take the rest of your night off."

"So should you."

She smiled at him, the lines around her eyes deep, her mouth tense. "It's just getting worse, Artie. Gimme the go ahead to check Greg out."

"No. Let me talk to him first, okay? We did a lot of digging already."

Hell, he'd looked at everything in Greg's file a million times during that first case. This wasn't going to be something they found on paper.

"Yeah, yeah, okay. But if he gives you names, call me ASAP and I'll start running them."

"You got it."

Quiet descended as Leah left, the last of the team that was getting too damned accustomed to working over Greg's store. The only thing left to do was clean up the damned elevator button so nothing ambushed Greg any more than it had to.

So he stood there with an alcohol-soaked cloth, swabbing. Avoiding going up there and telling Greg he had jack shit.

The elevator started rumbling, the ancient thing rattling and squeaking and rumbling. When it opened, Greg was there, wearing a pair of soaked shorts, eyes huge. "Artie?"

"Hey. Yeah. I was just." Procrastinating. Hiding his fucking disappointment. "We got it all cleaned up, I think." He stepped inside, holding himself away. "Except me. I need to wash up."

"Okay. Okay, upstairs. Shower. I... I made Duke a litter box and a little bed and brushed him and fed him and he seemed okay."

"He'll be fine. You didn't feed him anything with a wrapper, right?" He tried for humor. Fell short, but oh, well. The elevator took forever. He wanted to touch Greg, but not with blood and all on his hands.

"No. I fed him cream and warmed up tuna fish. I didn't try to eat. I just took a shower and did normal stuff." Greg jabbered, fluttered, got the elevator door open, and herded him into the apartment. "Put your clothes in the washer here, and I'll turn the water on for you and open the door."

"Thanks, babe." What else could he say? Suddenly he was bone damned tired. Exhausted. He stripped right off and padded naked to the shower.

The stark white bathroom was lit up - lights and candles and incense -- the steam already starting to billow from the shower. "I tried it with the lights down. I couldn't. This is better. Hop in. There's soap and everything."

Yeah. He stepped right in, nudging the soap off the shelf with his elbow and catching it, starting to scrub. He'd take the fucking skin right off before he felt clean, though.

It wasn't long before Greg's hands moved on his back, a soft, pained groan mingling with the splash of the water. He went to turn around, but Greg stopped him. "Don't. Not yet. I just need to help you get clean. I need to know you're okay."

There was pain in Greg's voice, tears.

God. Artie stood there, letting Greg touch him, wash him. "I'm sorry, babe. I'm fine. It's--" He stopped. It wasn't okay. Not one damned bit.

"I know. I know. Shh. You don't have to lie. I'm right here."

"Oh. Greg." He didn't lean, not on the slick tile, but he let Greg touch and soothe and heal something inside. Eventually Greg turned him around, pulled him close and just held on, face hidden in his throat.

Artie squeezed right back, just letting the water wash over them. He needed the contact, the closeness. It didn't fix it, didn't make the horror right, but it made things better, made the hollowed-out sensation in him easier.

The water ran cold before they were ready to move, and they staggered out, grabbing towels and mopping off. Artie headed straight for his chair, pulling Greg down with him. Greg settled the quilt around them, tucking them into the space, making it warm and dark and quiet.

Quiet was good.

Nuzzling Greg's throat was better.

"I'm sorry, man."

"We didn't do it. We're okay." Greg relaxed, snuggled in. "Even Duke's okay."

"Duke's probably way better than we are. He had cream." They should eat. He just didn't feel like it at all.

"We'll eat later. Fruit and pancakes. I just want this now."

"Me, too." Stroking Greg's back, he loved on him, held him. There'd be time for everything else later. For right now, he wouldn't think.

Neither of them would.

Chapter Eight

The phone rang at her desk and Virginia raced to reach it, heels click-clacking as she slid across the newsroom, hurrying as she stared at the clock. Two P.M. Christ. Christ. Don't hang up. Don't hang up.

Three days in a row. Three days, two P.M.

The biggest story in her fucking career, and she might miss a call because her goddamn pantyhose had gotten a runner.

"Hello?"

"Virginia?"

"Yes. Yes, sorry. How are you?"

"Fine. Our friend's place of business was crawling with police yesterday evening. I was surprised, not to hear it on the news. I think they were calling the killer The Collector."

"Oh, man. No. I hadn't heard. No one had. Dr. Pearsall has friends in the police force."

The man's voice was deep, knowing. "He does indeed. Do your job, Virginia, dear."

"Oh, I will. I will. I. Uh. I don't suppose you want to meet in person?" Something so she could get more from her mysterious source.

"I most definitely want to meet in person, dear. I'll call tomorrow."

"But... I..."

The phone went dead and Virginia scribbled in her awkward shorthand everything she'd learned over the last three days about Greg Pearsall, the book store he owned, the crimes he'd helped the Raleigh PD solve. Wicked. Now she could blow the case open. She had a nickname. The Collector.

And that cunt in the anchor chair said she'd never be more than a glorified weathergirl. Fuck that.

She grabbed the phone book. New Age. New Age. Come on, she knew it had to be in there.

***

Artie went back to the precinct and Greg started cleaning.

He closed the shop, he took the phone off the hook, he called the household supply place , and he started working. He steamed the carpets and bleached the walls. Had Mitch take everything out of his office and sent away. The windows, the cash register, the stairs -- if he couldn't make it clean, he made it empty so that girl's screams couldn't find him.

Once the downstairs was done, he started with his loft. Laundry, floors, sinks, light fixtures -- all cleaned. Dishes soaked in boiling bleach water. The music blared, and he had every light on.

That *thing* could not have his house.

Not.

Even the phone was cleaned. Which was a good thing, as it rang as soon as he put the handset on the cradle, startling him into a near panic.

He blinked, looked at it like it was a snake. Poisonous.

He picked it up, ready to tear it from the wall and throw it if the voice on the other end was... unfriendly.

"What?"

"Hey." He sagged a little. Artie. "I was just -- Well, I, uh. How are you?"

"Cleaning." Not sleeping. Panicking. Worrying. Normal stuff. "You?"

"I was just thinking about you, is all." Worrying, wondering, getting brain waves. Artie did that, called him when he was right at the edge of locking himself in the bathroom for a year.

"I'm here. I only have the outside stairs left to do. I'm doing them tonight."

"I'll come down. I don't like you out there alone." No, Artie wouldn't like that, as protective and stubborn as he was.

He nodded. "Are you sure?"

Yes, Artie. Please. It's... it's so *empty*.

"Yeah. Leah and I, well, we've got a ton of pictures to go through, and she said she'd take them home. Mug shots for that deadly assault last week. She doesn't mind." Artie laughed, a little hollow over the phone. "Besides, the cap says your thing is a priority."

"My thing? You need a nap, Artie, you sound tired." He wasn't sleeping. Never again.

"It's been a long day. Your case, Greg. The last package elevated it to a murder case for sure."

"Yes. Yes. I know. I. I can't think about that right now. I can't. I'm sorry."

"I know, babe. I know. Look, let me come by after this shift. Wait to clean until then. Promise me." So sure. So demanding. It was comforting in a way.

"I promise. No going outside. You'll use your key?"

"Yes. Don't you dare leave it unlocked." There was a hint of humor at last, Artie chuckling.

"No. If you want me, you'll have to come in and find me." He actually smiled, really smiled.

"I will. Give me an hour or so. I'll come." Artie always came. Always.

"I'll be here. Making the bed." Cleaning. Hiding.

Sort of like always.

***

His eyes were so tired they were blurry. Artie had to try the key three times, but he made it finally, stumbling into Greg's place, blinking hard at the overwhelming smell of bleach.

"Greg?"

"In the kitchen." God, the place was spotless, painfully so. He walked in on Greg scrubbing the ceiling tiles, arms and hands raw and lobstered, the entire room sparkling.

"You think it might be clean?" God, his head started throbbing, his nose twitching.

"I hope so. I want it to." Greg looked down at him, eyes blood-shot and shadowed. Exhausted. "I didn't clean outside."

"Good. How about I do it? I know I'm a slob, but my momma taught me to scrub." Fuck if he wanted Greg to get more blistered than he was.

"You look so tired." Greg blinked at him, the motion so slow Artie thought he could hear the click. "The bed is clean."

"Yeah? We can clean the outside. Later. I want you to wash off the bleach, though." His own head was spinning. "You're all blistered."

The rag dropped, those poor hands upturned toward him. "I didn't want to feel him anymore, Artie."

"Oh, babe." Artie grabbed Greg, raw hamburger skin and all, pulling him over and wrapping around him. "I wish I knew why this was happening to you."

Greg nodded, curling in with a little sigh. "I know. I do, too. I do, too."

He stroked Greg's hair, humming, his eyes closing. God, it felt good to stop. Just to stop going.

He got another nod. "Yes. Yes. I don't think I can sleep, but I can rest. You can sleep."

"We'll try it. Come on, babe." He was so tired. He should be starving, but the thought of food made him kinda nauseated. He pulled Greg toward the bed, his brain on autopilot.

The bed was covered in white sheets, white blankets. "No food. I'll hold you."

"Okay." He hoped Greg would sleep. Maybe they should go to his place after they had a little nap. Maybe Greg could sleep there.

"Duke would like that." Greg started undressing him, head bowed. "Tell me what happens next."

"I don't know. We have to start." Looking into your past. Digging up all your ghosts. Artie sighed.

Greg blinked, stepped away from him. "Why? I didn't do this."

"I know." Damn, sometimes that touch worked against him. "It's just, where else do we start?" He spread his hand helplessly.

"I don't want people looking at me. I don't like people looking at me. Calling me." The panicked look was creeping in. He knew it.

"No. Not going to be calling you. It's a standard background check. Has anyone in your life ever gone to jail, or set a cat on fire. It's okay." It was invasive as hell, but not directly. They wouldn't *talk* to Greg.

"No?" Greg searched his eyes, but didn't reach for him. "They... they should ask Duke. Duke would know if there were cat haters."

"Duke knows all." He wanted Greg to touch him, to see how he'd protect him from all of it if he could. No way was he gonna push it, though. Never. "Maybe we should sleep in the chair?"

"Yeah. Then food. Then your house. I want to go be at your house for a while." Greg grabbed his wrist, so cute and pouty and... "I am not petulant."

"I said pouty." Or thought it. God. Relief surged through him. "My house. Sounds good. We might even eat. Let your place air out."

The chair looked the same. Inviting.

"I don't have to clean it. You're sunk all in it. Your chair." Greg sounded almost drunk. "Your chair. God, my head hurts. Lemon-scented bleach sucks."

"Yeah. Yeah, but it's better than old Clorox." They flopped down. Somewhere he had a thought that they should vent the place or something. But he was too damned sleepy to carry through, just curling up with Greg, wrapping around him.

"Shh. No dreams. No dreams. Sleeping. No dreams."

"Okay. Okay, no dreams, babe. Sleep." Yeah.
Sleep. Artie sank into it like a stone in water.
Sleep.

The rest would just have to wait.

***

They hadn't napped long, the smell of the house
too overwhelming, so Greg had let Artie pack him
a bag for a couple of nights and they'd headed to
the little apartment and Duke. It was actually
comforting, sitting on Artie's sofa with Duke curled
in close, listening to Artie order pizza. Listening to
Artie just sort of thrum all around him.

"You okay?" Artie had hung up, and Greg
hadn't even noticed. Both Artie and Duke were
kind of purring.

"Better now." He was leaning, able to smile, to
relax, finally. He should have asked to come
earlier.

A kiss was his reward for that. "Good. Smells
better here."

"Smells like you." Duke started kneading dough
on his leg, blue eye rolling. "What kind of pizza
did you get?"

"I got two. One with fresh tomatoes and
mushrooms, and one Noah's Ark." What a name
for an all meat pizza. Artie loved it.

"Sounds good." He leaned to nuzzle Artie's jaw,
just breathe a minute. He could feel Artie's conflict
-- the need to work mixed with the need to stop and
rest.

"Yeah. Yeah, it'll be... I need some food. So do
you." Artie leaned a little harder, hand moving on
his hip, just idly stroking. "Rough week."

It came out as a sort of half snort, half chuckle.

"Yes. Truly shitty." He kissed again, humming. "Who is looking into my past? Leah? I mean, I was a professor. I fell down. I was in a coma. I bought a book store."

"It's Leah, yeah. She's good." Artie paused, and he heard the wheels spinning. "I don't expect we'll find anything. But if a former colleague has gone nutso or something, it will be something to go on."

"I guess. I mean, biology professors aren't known for their rages."

"I know. But there has to be something." Something to explain why it was him, because Artie didn't want it to be random, he wanted something they could trace, and where was that damned pizza?

"It's coming. You'll find it. You will." Sudden flashes of one unsolved case after another flooded him, the information just pouring in.

"I hope so." A sigh lifted his cheek where it rested on Artie's chest. "So. You want to take Duke on in checkers?"

He nodded, pushing himself upright, fingers brushing Artie's pen, a flash of the precinct office hitting him, the missing girls on the walls. "The second one on the right."

"Huh?" Halfway up off the couch, Artie turned back to stare at him. "What where?"

He reached for the pen, held it. "On the wall. By the light switch. The second one near the top. With the blue dress. She's one. And the coffee smells horrible and... there's something missing. Somebody took something and you noticed and forgot."

"Took something." Now Artie was back, kneeling in front of him, hands hovering but not touching. "From my office? From the scene? What?"

He shook his head. "Something you saw. You wondered, for a second and then forgot. Somebody *took* it."

"Damn. I wish I knew. So the girl. She's the one you saw the first night?"

"Yes. I couldn't see her before, not straight from the photo, but you were sitting down."

"Okay. Okay, what else, babe? Anything?" There were no leading questions; Artie was grasping at straws now.

"No... Your notebook. Your notebook. Your notebook. You left your pen on your desk." He could see blunt fingers. Coarse fingers. Scarred. Gray. Dark. "Someone wrote in your notebook, right there. Like he was meant to be there."

"My notebook?" Confusion. Plain old head scratching. "Someone was there in my office?"

"In the office. At the desk. Writing."

"Babe, I don't understand. If it's not me...I have my notebook. I would swear I do." Artie went to rummage through his coat pockets.

"It's not you. These are big fingers, course. Clumsy. You write in circles."

"It's not here. Fuck. I write in what?" Arms up on the coat rack, Artie looked under his armpit. Duke gave a delicate sneer.

"Circles. Curly-qs. These are deep slashes." He wrote in the air, demonstrating.

"Oh. Goddamn." The little cell phone was slipped out of Artie's coat, flipped open, and dialed in seconds. "Leah, honey? Do you have my notebook?"

The doorbell rang and Greg went to answer it, opening his wallet to nudge money out so he didn't have to touch it.

"There you go." The kid had a face like a pizza. Goodness. Artie muscled him out of the way and took the boxes just before his hands touched them.

"Thank you. Goodnight." Go away. We're busy.

The door clicked shut, Artie taking the pizza over to the table. "No? Shit. No, it's gone. Greg thinks someone...uh-huh. Okay. Thanks. Bye."

"I'm sorry." He hated giving bad news.

Duke, on the other hand, was *stalking* the pizza.

"It's okay. I swear to God, Duke, if you eat all of the andouille I will skin you alive." Plates, napkins, forks. "You want a Coke?"

"I do. Do you have a safe glass?"

Although Artie's house was growing safer, Artie's presence less and less unusual.

"Uh-huh. I uh." Artie blushed bright. "I stole your 'name the microbe' one."

"Oh." He grinned, the whole pen-picture-notebook bullshit easing up. "Yeah? Excellent, detective."

"It seemed like a good idea. I took your blue plate, too." Oh, the sneaky bastard. The sound of a pizza box opening made him look around. Duke sat a good two feet away from the table, looking nonchalant. Greg wondered if he had telekinesis.

It wasn't as strange as it sounded.

"Did you know cats can't taste sweets?"

"Really? They sure can taste sausage." He got a grin and a peck on the nose before Artie set them up for supper.

"I used to eat at this little Cajun place -- before. It was amazing, the sausages they made." He sat at the table, hands flat on the wood, listening to Artie.

"Yeah? I like the sausages at this one deli. Man, they do them all. Duke, I swear to God if you don't leave that alone..." When he looked this time, Duke was poking delicately at the pizza crust with one set of claws, having moved like lightning.

He patted his lap, inviting Duke to share. He wasn't worried, no matter what Artie said. "We should get some; jambalaya is a fabulous thing."

"We should. Some rice, some heavy spice." Artie glared at the cat on his lap before sitting down and handing over a wad of napkins. "Watch it, he's a messy eater."

He nodded, tearing half a slice off and setting it down on a napkin for Duke, then digging in. "What did Leah say about your notebook? Did she have it?"

"No. She said she'd check, though, make sure she hadn't just picked it up without thinking." Artie chewed enthusiastically, licking cheese off his lower lip.

He knew better. Someone had it. Someone had written on it. He turned his attention back to the pizza, listening to Duke purr and rumble against his thigh. Why a kidney? Kidneys weren't easy to remove, really. Weren't like a heart. Weren't sexual...

"Hey. You in there?" He'd heard Artie's voice like a distant hum, but he started when Artie touched his hand.

He blinked, *Artie* in his head, sudden and sure and sharp. "Yes. Yes. Oh."

Greg forgot, sometimes, the way everyone touched. How he'd missed it.

"Is this okay?" They'd had sex, they'd slept together, but Artie still worried about touching him casually. That told Greg so damned much about how Artie felt, made the whole mess go away for a minute.

"Yeah." His cheeks hurt, his smile was so big. Yeah, more than okay.

"Oh, cool." They sat there and grinned at each other until Duke hissed and spat and sank his teeth into Artie's hand.

"Now, now. Don't bite the hand that feeds you. All you had to do was ask." Greg fed Duke another half-piece, trying not to grin as Artie cussed.

"I swear I ought to make a hand warmer out of that cat." Artie and Duke stared each other down, Duke's one-eyed look way more intimidating than Artie's tired cop face. Then Artie hooted and cracked a grin. "Asshole."

"He's a lover." Not as big of one as Artie, but close. He scratched that sensitive spot at the base of Duke's tail and leaned to lick a drop of sauce off Artie's bottom lip. Both of them, Duke and Artie, purred for him, sounding so in tune he could have sung along. It was hilarious. Greg thought maybe he could get used to it, being in the middle of those sounds.

"Mmm." Artie broke free from the kiss that had evolved out of his simple touch, stroking Greg's cheek. "Damn. Pizza's a good taste on you."

"I'll have to remember that." He took a deep breath, relaxing - really relaxing-- for the first time in days.

"You do that." The lines around Artie's mouth and eyes eased, too, like Artie knew, and maybe he did. Maybe the man could read him better than Greg thought he could.

He nodded, fingers sliding in lazy circles on Artie's leg. Basking. He was basking. After a decade of not having this, he deserved a little time to bask. Damn it.

Artie seemed reluctant to break the silence after that, just touching him with one hand and eating with the other. It was easy, just to sit and blink and stare, to let his mind wander and listen to the slow hum of Artie's thoughts purring through him. Artie was a little worried and a lot tired, but he was more interested in thinking how good it felt to have Greg there and was wondering if Greg would hate his clutter or maybe if Duke would try to eat them like Godzilla kitty and oh, that was good pizza. Stream of consciousness stuff that made Greg smile.

"Does it bother you? That I can hear you?" He shifted, leaned more.

"Huh?" Artie frowned a minute, thoughts scattering like pigeons in front of a church. Then Artie figured it out and shook his head. "Nah. I mean, it's part of you."

"That it is. You should have seen me, when I woke up with it. I couldn't stop screaming."

The crust of pizza Artie held plopped back to the paper plate, and the man grabbed his hand again, thumb rubbing, trying to ease him. "I bet. That had to suck like a Hoover, man."

He chuckled. "Not to put too fine a point on it, yes. Yes, it did. But the alternative was dead or in a coma, so..."

"Well, I'm glad you aren't either. In either. Whatever. You done?" Tapping the pizza box, Artie looked from him to Duke.

"Yeah. There enough for a late-night snack?" He was all about the crawling out of bed and noshing.

"You know it. And if we close up now Duke won't get any more hair on it." That caused Artie and Duke to growl at each other again, the big cat hopping off Greg's lap and stalking off, looking offended.

"You two are made for each other, I swear to God." He took his free-lap opportunity to shift and settle in Artie's lap.

"Oh, now, this is much better." Artie laughed. "I do love that stupid cat, but I would much rather have you like this. You touch nicely."

"Yeah? I haven't forgotten how?" He chuckled, fingers sliding over the line of nerves down the center of Artie's chest.

"Nope. And you don't have claws." Just that easily, Artie leaned in and kissed him, mouth on his soft, light. Tasting like pizza sauce.

Greg just let himself touch, hands memorizing each group of muscles, each inch of skin, first on top of Artie's T-shirt, then beneath. God. It was so *good* to feel the way Artie responded.

"Mmmhmm. Yum." He hadn't said anything out loud, but Artie said it for him, touching him back. Those blunt fingers slid over his cheeks and chin, over his collarbones and down over his ribs. It made him gasp, made him shudder as the input from Artie eased, the sensation of those hands taking over.

"That's it. Just feel, Greg. Just feel." They kissed again, Artie's tongue pushing deep, really tasting him.

His fingers tangled in Artie's hair, bodies held together, shoulder to hip. He wasn't even sure he was hard; he just knew that he was feeling. One of Artie's hands slid behind his back, pulling him closer, fingers stroking the bumps of his spine. Each little touch made him shiver. He arched and moaned, hips sliding on Artie's thighs, the rasp of fabric against skin delicious. Artie loved on him, lips sliding down his throat, the heavy growth of Artie's whiskers adding another layer of sensation. Wonderful.

"Oh. More. Show me more." He chuckled at the murmured greed, the pleasure at his words belying the grumble.

"Uh-huh. We need to. Can I?" Artie tugged at his clothes. "These. Off."

"Uh-huh." He managed to get his shirt off, then Artie's, eyes rolling as their bellies met.

That was just-- Yeah. Artie reached between them, stroking him, calluses catching on the short hairs below his navel. His body just ached, muscles going tight, cock pushing up to try to catch Artie's attention. It worked. Artie touched him through the cloth of his pants, then with nothing in between as one big hand pushed under, closing around him. His eyes tried to roll back as Artie stroked up from the base, giving him some friction.

His own hands got stuck, holding onto Artie's shoulders, bracing himself against the pleasure that poured over him.

"Yeah. Yeah. Oh, God, you're hot." He could feel it sharply for just a moment, Artie's surge of pleasure at the feel of his skin, of his heat. His eyes flew open, the sensation of Artie's hand and Artie's pleasure crashing together in his head, sending him flying.

"Kiss me, Greg. Please." Leaning, Artie pulled at him, savored him, fingers sliding over the heat of his cock. One fingertip pushed into his slit.

His thighs went hard as rocks and he dove into the kisses, tongue pushing in, tasting Artie, fucking Artie. Arching up under him, Artie grunted, rocking the chair beneath them, making it squeak. That kiss was going to just devour him. One of them got Artie's jeans open, he wasn't sure which one, and then his pants were shoved down, their hands meeting around their cocks, pulling and tugging furiously.

It was fast after that, hard and fast and good, making them pant and grunt, and it was sort of amazing how quickly it went from a friendly pizza to you-now-yeah. Artie squeezed, pushing all the way down to his balls before pulling back up, forcing Greg's hand to follow, and then Artie was coming, shaking and groaning, the man's hot come spilling over Greg's hand. He thought he might never be able to feel Artie shoot without giving it up himself, balls aching as his prick throbbed.

"Oh. Oh, Greg. Yeah." Artie leaned against him, forehead to his.

"Uh-huh." He nodded, blinked. Watched. "Yeah."

"Well. That was a hell of a dessert. What should we do for a snack later?"

Greg licked his lips, thinking about how it would feel, Artie's cock sliding in and out of his lips. "I bet I can think of something."

Chapter Nine

Virginia pulled into the parking lot of the bookstore and drove toward the back, looking at the big old building with the stained bricks, the crystal ball sign. She could so buy that a psychic worked here. Lived here.

A professor? Not so much. It was a little scary, with the tattoo parlor and cleaners and deli and all. Still, it was the morning, so how scary could it be?

She tied up her hair in a ponytail, hoping it made her look as young to strangers as it did to her own eyes.

Okay. Go in. Play interested shopper. See if she could get in to see the owner. Lalala.

There was a heavy older lady behind the counter, grinning at her. Nodding. "Morning, honey. Welcome to The Candle's End. Are you looking for something in particular?"

A psychic, gay ex-biology professor with a serial killer friend? Something so I can keep my exclusive? "No. No, I was just curious."

"That's usually where everything starts. If you have any questions, holler."

"Thanks. I will." The place was neat, in that vaguely incensey, New Agey weirdo way. Lots of books. Lots of random shiny things. She found a little rose carved from a pink stone on a chain and grinned. Her sister would like that for Christmas. She took it back to the counter.

"Will this be all?"

"Yeah. Yeah, it will. Is this your store?" She dug a twenty out of her purse, handed it over.

"Hmm? Well, I own a part of it. Greg owns the lion's share and the building."

"Does he work the store, too?" Would this place make that kind of money?

"Sometimes. We have flexible schedules. $16.73." The necklace was packaged up, handed over, the friendly smile turning a little suspicious. "Have a good day."

Damn it.

"Yeah. Yeah, you, too." She headed outside, cussing a little under her breath. She was going to have to figure that whole subtle-questioning thing out. Her cell phone rang, the private number not showing up on her phone at all. "Yeah?"

"Virginia?"

"Yeah? Who is this?"

"Nobody important." The blow to her head was sharp and sudden, and her knees hit the ground before she even knew what happened, the world spinning.

"I don't like your hair like that, dear."

***

"Leah? Babe? Are you sure you don't have my notebook? Shit. Okay, well, I'll see you at the office in about fifteen."

Against his better judgment, but also feeling it was the safest thing, Artie had left Greg at his place. Asleep. With an admonition to Duke to watch over the man and not eat all the leftover pizza. Not that Artie could blame him. The last few days had sucked the proverbial donkey balls. Sighing, Artie pulled into the Amoco next to the station to buy coffee, Danish, and a new spiral bound notebook.

At least he still had his pen.

At the last minute he bought Leah a chocolate milk and one of those healthy breakfast sandwich things. That girl never ate enough for two.

He wandered in, scratching at the spot his tie was rubbing raw already, his bag getting soggy as coffee leaked out into it. "Hey, honey," he said to Leah. "Whatcha got?"

"Man, did you know the doc was like some biggie-wow before he got hurt? Big money. Big news. Man got his Ph.D. at twenty, got tenure at twenty-four. Lived with a pianist who is now making the cash." She chewed on a cherry blo-pop, grinning at the chocolate milk. "No record. No trouble. Just the accident - Greg fell down three flights of stairs after a late night class. Students found him."

"And we're sure it was an accident?" Really, weirder things had happened in academia than someone pushing their prof down the stairs. Artie had investigated a double at NC State at one point, where a cute little sorority chick had killed a prof and his wife...

"No, but if it wasn't, no one found anything. Greg lost three months, between the injury, the coma and all. I called the ex. Not the nicest fella you'll ever meet; said Doc had gone bugnuts crazy, that the accident ruined him and that's why they broke up. Man didn't even know where Greg was."

Artie felt the hot flush crawling up his neck. Probably a good thing Greg's ex didn't live in the same town. Artie might go beat him a little. Or maybe a lot. "So much for standing by your man, huh? Man, your ankles are huge."

"Fuck you, man." She tossed the milk cap at him, eyes rolling. "I have talked to family, friends, people he works with. Besides being weird, the biggest thing I'm finding is that the couple at the store with him grow pot in the basement."

"Oh, the horror." Grinning, Artie put Leah's sandwich in the microwave, heating up his own Danish by putting it over his steaming coffee. He wasn't big on busting people for small personal crops. "Well, that doesn't help us."

"Nope. I'll start on the other professors next, but Artie, why would someone come for him now and not then? Then he was something to compete against. Now? Can you imagine him digging into a dead thing and cutting it open?" Leah turned a little green all of a sudden, pale as anything. "Oh. Oh, blah."

Bless her heart. She ran for the bathroom, and Artie mulled it over, munching his Danish and flipping out the little pristine notebook and frowning. Something was weird. Something he should have noticed kept... poking.

"Better?" he asked when Leah came back, handing her the little plate. "That's what you get for all that sugar."

"Shut up, asshole." She chuckled, grinned, and settled back down. "Well, what do we know? We know he's local. We know he knows Greg's store, the phone there." She tilted her head. "Has he gotten calls at the apartment?"

"Nope. At least not that I know of. There was the garbage thing. And, well, it's gonna sound crazy, but I'm missing my notebook."

"Missing it? You didn't find it?" Leah frowned, started looking through the drawers.

"No. And Greg..." Well, Leah had believed before he did, but that didn't mean he didn't feel weird talking about it. "He said someone was writing in it."

"Someone who?" Leah started digging shit out, muttering. "Someone in here? A leak? What?"

"I don't know. I got the impression that he thought it was our guy." And it creeped him right the hell out.

"Here?" Leah's face went hard, stiff. "You go get him, Artie. Bring him here and sit his ass down and make him do his thing. It's not a cop doing this, not one of us."

His back went right up. "There's no guarantee I lost the notebook here. It could have been at the coffee shop or in Greg's shop or someplace..." He didn't want to bring Greg to the station. God, it would make Greg sick as a dog.

"Did he know? Did he say?" Leah stood up, started walking, pacing.

"No. He said..." Artie thought hard. "He said he was writing in it. That my writing was different."

"Let's go see Greg." He knew that voice, that tone. Greg was fucked.

"He's at my place, Leah. I don't want my place to be a bad thing. I want it to be safe." He just couldn't do that to Greg. He couldn't.

"Your place? Like staying there?" Put those eyebrows down, girl.

"It was tough, staying at his place. There was bleach..." He hated explaining. Artie sighed. "Look, he has an easier time seeing things again where he saw them. Why don't I get him and meet you at the shop?"

"Okay. I'm not trying to fuck with him, Art. I just... We're on what? Vic three? The press catches this and Greg'll never sleep again."

"I know. I know. I just..." Like to keep Greg's life as normal as possible? Like to keep him sane? Artie sighed. "I'll meet you there, honey."

"I tell you what; I'll meet you at lunch. Let y'all get settled."

"Okay. Yeah. Okay. In between I'll make some calls, retrace my steps. See if anyone found my notebook."

"I'll bring chicken and salad. It's not one of us, Art. It can't be."

"No. No, you're right. No one would do this. That kidney. It was perfectly removed, babe. It was...well, you saw it." She turned green again, and Artie apologized, hand on her shoulder as he got up. "Okay, it's a plan. I'm gonna go. Get Greg."

"Okay. I'll be at the store at noon. Here's the forensic reports and the missing persons photos."

"Thanks, babe." He grinned at her, rubbing her belly like a Buddha for good luck. "See you."

Now he had to go break it to Greg that they wanted him to perform like a circus freak.

Fun.

Well, maybe he could start the conversation with offering to bring Greg to the station. That always worked *so* well.

Then make it seem like he was being magnanimous by going to the shop instead. On the way home Artie called all of his usual haunts, asking about his notebook. Nada.

He rubbed his neck as he made his way to his door, key fitting into the lock. God, he hated this shit. Greg was worth it. He was. But damn.

Duke was squalling up a storm as soon as the door opened, hackles risen, single eye just spitting fire.

He could hear the answering machine whirring, the end of a conversation just audible. "...you have a moment for an interview? We've contacted Mr. Pearsall at his store and his home. Is it true he's assisting another investigation?"

Oh, Jesus fuck. Nudging Duke aside with his leg, Artie went looking. "Babe? Greg? Where are you, man?"

"They've been calling for the last hour. I told Alice to not tell them anything. She says one came in this morning, digging." Greg was dressed, lips tight and hard. "I guess I need to go home. It won't help you if someone finds me here."

Artie shifted from foot to foot, debating on the whole touching thing. He wanted to. Then he said a mental fuck it and held out a hand. It was the right fucking decision, Greg's hand sliding into his just like that, holding on. Artie pulled him close, hugging tight. "We need to go to the shop anyway. Goddamn those fucking reporters."

"Amen. How do they find all this out?"

"Hell if I know, babe. Leah is pretty adamant that it's not someone in the precinct." Artie wasn't so sure, at least about the press. The other shit, no, he didn't think was a cop. But the damned reporters always knew.

"I'm not going to your desk again, and I didn't say it was a policeman, did I?"

"No. She just thinks because of my notebook...where did I leave it that he got it, Greg?" He could feel the tension grow, could feel Greg start to vibrate.

"Give me your pen." Those fingers closed around it, Greg muttering about the Danish not getting hot and Leah's ankles and him signing his name on a credit card slip.

Artie watched him closely. Where had he signed a card slip that he might have taken the notebook out, too? If his pen had been hooked in it...

Greg paced, working back, day after day. There was his shower. The pizza. The bleach.

The kidney.

Artie swallowed against bile, that memory sharp and clear in his own mind, that and how he'd hoped to spare Greg some of it.

Greg went to the window, head on the glass, panting. "You were at a meeting. There were photos. Leah was there. It was the morning; you hated the coffee. You wrote on a folder and thought about your book."

Shit. Artie went still, his mind racing. That was. Fuck a duck. It was at the station. He'd had it before the meeting, but Leah had rushed him into that interrogation room...

"Fuck."

"No. No. He picked up the pen and he wrote things in your book. The desk is scarred, people saw him. People saw him there, Artie."

Oh. Oh, hell, yes. Okay. That was good. Greg looked green. Artie went over and put a hand on his arm. "You okay, babe?"

"Don't touch me. I can't... I." Greg's eyes met his, angry and hurt. "It's about me. It's about me somehow. He knows. How can he know? I don't."

Damn it.

Artie pulled his fingers away for like, half a second. Then he let out an explosive curse and grabbed Greg tight, holding on, just holding. "I dunno. We'll figure it out."

Greg gasped, then his pen clattered to the ground as the man pushed close. "Artie."

"Got you." Goddamn, what a mess. But if someone saw the guy. Shit, this could be it.

"You need to go, huh? To the station?" Greg's forehead rested on his chin.

"Shit. Yeah, and I need to call Leah. Tell her not to meet us at the shop. She needs to get the camera footage from that day." Holding Greg with one arm, Artie pulled out his cell, hoping to catch Leah before she left.

"Okay. I'm going to get my shoes and go home." Greg kissed his jaw, slipped out from under his arm, and headed back into the bedroom.

"Wait..." Artie made a grab, missed, and cussed up a storm as Duke's teeth sank into his ankle.

"What do you need, Art?" Leah asked when the call connected. "I'm on a call with this crazy Russian professor guy."

"It was at the station, Leah. He says it was at the station. Probably at my desk. While we were in that meeting with Lymon. Someone probably saw him." He shook his leg. Duke held. Goddamn it.

"At your desk? I don't believe it. This Russian dude says lots of folks hated the doc. Lots of faculty."

"Get your head out of your ass, Leah. I'm not saying it was a cop. Maintenance, janitorial. The mailman. And I imagine people did. Greg's fucking smart." He made another grab as Greg went by again, Duke hampering him at every step.

"And aggravating. Cocky, too. And I flaunted my lover every chance I got. Wore pride T-shirts to class. Failed a lot of jocks and idiots. Tell Leah not to forget that. Students hated me." Greg shrugged on a jacket. "Everyone hated me back then. Now I'm harmless."

"I think she's pretty aggravated with you right now, babe. Jesus fucking Christ, Duke, if you don't let me go, I'm going to make a pillow out of you. Leah, I need tapes. Greg, you just fucking hold on a minute." Artie just exploded. He was Not Happy.

Duke let go and Leah hung up and Greg just stood there by the door, looking pinched and tight all over.

"I'm sorry." Artie dropped the phone in his pocket, pretty sure he was talking to Greg and not Duke, but who knew? "Just, please. C'mere a minute, okay?"

"You..." Greg nodded, took half a step toward him. "It's okay, detective. I'm okay."

Artie took the rest of the steps. "You're a rotten liar. I'll give you a ride." He put his arms around Greg and held on. This had been, well, not easier before. But not as personal. He couldn't protect Greg all the time. But he wanted to.

"And promise me you won't wander, okay?"

"I'll try not to." Greg leaned into him, sighed a little. "I haven't had a lot of opportunity to lie lately. I'm out of practice."

He let his hand rise to rest between Greg's shoulder blades, stood for a minute feeling Greg's heart thump against his chest. Then he nodded. "Yeah. We'll figure this out, Greg. I promise."

They had to get going. Damn.

"Then let's go. You have work to do."

"Yeah. I do." He wanted to ask if it was okay to come see Greg tonight, but he was afraid he'd push the man too far. "Come on, babe. We've got a psycho to catch."

"I'll leave the backdoor unlocked for you."

Artie bit back his growl. "Can I just call you when I get there, man? I'd rather not take any chances."

"Protective ass." Greg kissed him, full on the mouth.

"Mmmhmm." He just let the kiss go long and sweet, licking Greg's lips.

That got rid of that last bit of pinched and unhappy, Greg relaxing into him, breathing. Nodding. "Let's go. It's good. We're good."

"Okay. Yeah." They'd make it good. Damn it. Artie led the way, knowing it was going to be a long damned day.

"They always are, but you'll find him."

"We will. Together. Count on it."

Chapter Ten

It takes all night, all night, but finally he is finished. The third floor is destroyed, but sacrifices have to be made for art.

He has redecorated, just for his professor.

"Anatomy is not a dead science, guys. The human form is beautiful in its symmetry, in its complexity."

Symmetry.

He takes one backgammon piece from the board, replaces it, the bright pink polish on the toenail chipped a little from when she'd struggled. Fought.

If only she'd listened to him.

Then his offering would be perfect.

Shame.

He will simply have to try again.

***

Artie dropped Greg off at the store and made it to the station without giving into road rage and shooting some innocent bystander. It was a near thing. But he did it. Go him.

He slammed in, yanking at his tie until it came loose, tossing it at his chair. "Whatcha got, Leah?"

"I'm running the tapes. So far, I haven't seen anything odd, but there's not a clear visual of your desk." Leah shifted, stretched. "How's the doc?"

"Not so hot. But he'll do. You want me to start looking at the logs?" Maintenance folks had to log in and out.

"Yeah. We know we're looking for a man, right? Doc give you an age?" She pushed over a huge log book.

"No. But he said someone saw him. Someone had to." Artie yanked off his jacket, too, and plopped down. "Damn, I hate this shit."

"You signed on for it, honey. Let's make the city safe for weird-assed psychic ex-professors and homeless blondes."

"Yeah, but combing papers..." He needed an intern or something. Did they let cops have interns? Artie started reading, looking at who all had been there that day.

There was something fucked up about the fact that he'd been at the precinct for damn near ten years and only recognized a few names - Harold and Vic were both the daytime janitors; Nancy, he thought, was that sweet lady who dealt with supplies...

"Who is Andy Bruckle?" he asked Leah. "And Louis Mayle?"

"Louis is that little contractor who's doing the files. The one with the lisp and all. I... I don't know a Bruckle."

Artie highlighted it with yellow. One for the look-into file. He kept scanning. There weren't many, but he'd check the day before and after, too, just in case someone filled in the wrong line.

Andy Bruckle. Nick Garza. That was a pretty damn short...

"Artie, look at this." Leah hit rewind, turned the screen toward him. There was a guy, shortish, wide shouldered, wearing a ball cap. The guy had on one of those huge belts, wires and tools dangling and shaking as he headed right for Artie's desk, bent over it.

He glanced over, then got up and went around to look at the monitor, watching as Leah rewound. "What am I looking for?"

"Watch your desk."

There was a pile of papers, pictures, a coffee cup. Then the guy leaned over and stood and walked off, leaving a clean desk.

"Shit. He took all my shit!" Artie didn't mean to sound so shocked, but how could someone just do that and not have anyone say anything?

"He did. What was there? What all was in that pile? Who the hell was that?"

"My notebook. Some of the files you gave me on the missing persons. I had some in the meetings." Shit. "Some shit on Greg. From the last case."

"Fuck."

Leah stood up, started pacing. "Okay, okay. I'll get with Mitch, see if he can't identify this guy. See if we can't get him in for questioning. What kind of shit on Doc?"

"Just the files from the case with some remarks on his involvement. Man," Artie watched the tape again, "he took my coffee cup."

His phone rang, startling him. Greg. Damn. "Artie? Artie, it's Alice. You need to come. You need to come right now."

"I'll be there in ten or less." Artie grabbed his jacket and headed for the door, not even glancing at Leah, trusting her to know where he was going.

"He... You need to. There are. Oh, God, Artie. There are things in the house. Upstairs. Parts."

He could hear her gagging, and damned if he didn't have a graphic mental picture of what it looked like. "Where's Greg, honey? How is he?"

"He's locked himself up on the roof. He turned the elevator off. I heard him tearing things apart upstairs and screaming. Now he's quiet. I've closed the store. That's okay, right?"

"Yeah, that's..." Okay? Fuck no, it wasn't okay. Greg could have hurt himself. He could have. God knew what. Artie hopped in the Camaro, barely looking before he squealed out of the lot.

He used the siren, speeding through lights and daring anyone - *anyone* -- to get in his way. "What... what do you want me to do, Artie? I'm... I'm not feeling a lot of love and light here."

"Just stay there until I get there, can you do that? And listen." And make sure Greg wasn't throwing himself off the roof. "And if you see anything out of place in the store, kind of note it down, but don't touch. Okay?"

"Okay. Okay. I can do that. Can I call Mitch? Have him come?"

"Yeah. I would feel better if he took you home." No one should be alone. Come on, come on. Artie took a corner on two wheels.

"'Kay. You... Greg can't stay in the apartment. You'll help him?"

"I will, I promise. I'm almost there, honey. Just hang in there." There. He could see the building.

"I will. I'm going to call Mitch." The line went dead as he pulled up in the alley, cussing violently as a news van pulled up in front about the same time. He took a second to call Leah. "Honey. You. Uniforms. Forensics. Greg's. Now. The press is already here."

"Motherfucker."

"Exactly."

Artie slammed the phone shut and got out of his car and flashed his badge. "Y'all need to leave. There's nothing for you here but a trip to the station for obstructing justice."

"This is a public place, detective." God, he hated that bitch from KXJS. "We have the right to be here. Is it true that Dr. Pearsall is assisting with an investigation?"

"No. You turn that camera on, son, and I'll bust it into a million pieces. Accidentally, of course." He bared his teeth. "You get in my way, you'll have a criminal record so fast your head spins."

He left them, the bitch opening and closing her mouth, the cameraman backing off a little, and that gave him just enough time to slip inside when Alice opened the door.

A huge potted plant landed on top of the news van, the crash the loudest fucking thing Artie'd ever heard. Apparently Greg agreed with him.

Poor Alice jumped a mile.

"Just the news people getting a taste of Greg's mood, honey. You'd best have Mitch meet you out front. And don't talk to anyone. Got it?"

"O...okay. Okay. You... you don't need me?" Another pot hit the ground, the reporters scrambling. Lord, lord.

"No, not now." He couldn't deal with both Alice and Greg at the same time. "I need you to write everything down when you get home, though. Everything. Okay?"

"Sure, Artie. Sure." A horn honked and she screamed a little, jumped. "That's Mitch. I'm going. I'm sorry. I have to."

"Okay, honey. Go on. Make a run for it and don't stop for anything." He handed her a card. "Call me if anything, and I mean anything, happens."

"'Kay." She kissed his cheek and ran as something else dropped -- part of the rose trellis, it looked like.

Greg was going to kill someone. Artie couldn't go up the stairs, he'd have to go outside, and God knew he didn't want to do that, so he went to the elevator and checked to see if Greg really had it blocked or if he could call it down.

He sighed as the damned thing started whirring, thankful again that Greg made him master keys to everything.

He made it up to Greg's place, stepping out carefully, not wanting to disturb anything more than he had to. And worried the man might start chucking things at him.

The apartment didn't look strange at all, not at the first glance. It was the second glance that he got sight of a thin, graceful arm, sitting as if posed, on a bookshelf.

Artie swallowed. Oh, fuck. Oh, Jesus, fuck. Artie couldn't look. Not now. He had to get Greg, had to get Greg out. Then he'd bring in a team, they'd sweep.

Other things caught his eye as he made it to the door, things he wasn't going to look at right then. First you protect the innocent. Then you clear the scene. Then you work it.

One step after another.

Greg first. Artie cautiously moved to the stairs, checking his danger areas, creeping up so as not to startle. He nudged the door open. "Greg?"

"Go away!" A chunk of roots and leaves and dirt hit the wall beside the door. Oh, lord. He hadn't gotten to see Greg in full-blown hysteria since the time he shoved the man into a packed elevator, way back when.

"Greg. Come on. It's Artie." He kept his voice calm, even, his movements slow. "Come on."

"He came into my *house*! Into my rooms! My place!" Greg's eyes were huge, wild, rolling.

"I...I saw." God. He swallowed again, the bile rising. He'd seen some pretty intense stuff in his career, but he'd slept here, eaten here. "Greg, we need to get you out of here, secure the scene. Uniforms are on their way. They'll clear out the reporters."

"I'm not going anywhere." Greg stepped away from him, shaking his head. "He touched things in my house."

"Greg, we have to process. There'll be people crawling all over." Greg would go nuts. More nuts. Whatever.

Greg groaned, the sound raw and agonized, head banging on the shed, over and over again. "No. No, this is my house. It was mine. I'll burn it down first."

"Greg." Fuck. Artie rubbed his chest, the sudden heartburn really getting to him. Damned

acid. "I'm sorry. I'm so sorry. I should've...we
should've. Done more. Left a uniform. I just
wanted to take you home, and I..."

Got too fucking wrapped up to do his
goddamned fucking job.

Greg stopped, looked over at him. "You're
sorry? You didn't bring this here. I did."

"But--" Spreading his hands, Artie looked
around, shrugged. "I'm supposed to protect and
serve, babe."

"I don't..." Greg sort of collapsed in on himself,
still standing, but smaller somehow, gray as
laundry water. "I'm sorry. I'll go. You have keys to
everything."

"Greg." Something was broken. Something he
didn't know if he could get back. He was gonna try
anyway. Artie reached out, just holding out his
hand. "Please."

"Please what? I don't... There are things in my
bed. Parts. In the kitchen. Everywhere." Greg
stepped forward, came toward him.

Thank God. Artie met him halfway. "I just. I
dunno. Need to touch you. Is that okay?" He wasn't
sure what would be okay. Ever. Was he being too
fucking dramatic?

"I'll hear you. All of you. I... My fucking head
hurts, Artie." Greg reached out, hand torn up and
shaking violently.

Well, his head had to be quieter than Greg's. He
was still stunned. Artie took Greg's hand, just
pulling the man to him, kissing the scraped fingers.
Putting all of his need to touch Greg into it and
nothing else, if that could even happen.

"Artie..." Greg's knees buckled, falling against
Artie and letting him hold them both up.

"I got you. I got you, babe." He wasn't a cop then. Just Greg's. Just there because the man needed him there.

"I was going to ask you to let me bring Duke here today for company. I'm glad I didn't."

"Yeah. I guess it was best. Okay." Fuck, he just didn't seem to know what to do next. It wasn't a feeling Artie liked or knew well. "What happened, babe? Can you tell me some while we wait for the uniforms?"

"I used the elevator and went upstairs, went in and got changed and then I went to make coffee. There was... there was a coffee cup. A strange coffee cup in the cupboard. I reached for it and there was a finger."

Oh, fuck. Okay, so they had a finger. And an arm. "What else?"

"There... there's a heart in my freezer. An eye in the iris vase, optical nerve attached. An arm. Chunks of flesh in the bed."

"All right. Stop." He could tell from the way the words were running together that Greg was close to losing it again. Artie heard sirens and then heard raised voices as the uniforms started clearing out the reporters.

"You need to work." Greg stepped back away from him, eyes rolling a little. "Can I stay up here?"

"Yes. Yeah. I mean, if you'd rather wait to leave until we clear. Leah will be here. She could take you..." That would go over like a lead balloon, with both Leah and Greg.

"No." Greg shook his head. "Do I have to give a statement to anyone?"

"I'll take it. Later. Do you... You need anything?" Artie rubbed at Greg's arms, soothing them both.

"No." Greg shook his head, skin gray as ash. "I don't need anything right now."

"Okay. Sit tight. Meditate or something." And, yeah, he knew how trite that was, but it was all he could offer. That and a kiss, as he had to go down and help out with the scene.

The crime scene folks were there, the uniforms keeping the press back. Leah was in the store, almost growling, eyes snapping.

"Is he okay, Art?"

"No. No, he's not. He found a finger in a coffee cup. How would you be?" He was taking it out on the wrong person and he knew it, but damn.

"Fuck off. How are we working this? He's going to have to go down to the station for a statement."

"I'll take his statement. Later. He's staying up there now, and not throwing anything else off." Artie hoped. "What have we got?"

"I haven't been up yet. Crime lab says Greg's place smells like bleach... Did he clean it?"

"Not this time. Last time. The bleach is left over from last time." Goddamn it. How many times did they have to go through this?

"Okay, how about Alice? Did she see anything? Is she still here?"

"She was having a breakdown, babe. I sent her home. I'll let you take her statement later, while it's still fresh, but she needs the hubby." He looked around now that he was braced, placing his feet carefully.

"Okay. Cool. So, what? He's watching, right? He's got to be watching. How do we play it?"

"If I knew..." Clear your fucking head, man, Artie thought. "Okay. We'll get what we can from this scene. We'll show Greg the tape, see if he can get anything from what little you can see of the guy. We talk to Alice, and we figure out where to stash Greg. He can't stay here."

"We're taking Greg to the station, then? I'll do it, if you want. Pop him in an interrogation room."

Artie rubbed the back of his neck. "What is it with you and this hard-on for putting Greg down at the station? You haven't seen him, Leah. He's teetering. He won't do us any good in a straightjacket."

"What am I supposed to do, Artie? He's a vic, a target. I'm supposed to plop him in front of his TV with bits of dead chick on it? If he needs to be hospitalized or sedated or whatever, he does. That's how this shit works."

"I know. He's different." Damn it. "Can we just work the scene?"

"Sure." Leah's lips went tight, and she started snapping orders to the random techs. "I want photos of the crowd. I want to know how much of a body we have. I want to know exactly where Dr. Pearsall was and what he touched, and I want that goddamn music turned *off*!"

He'd make it up to her. He would. Artie just squeezed her shoulder as she went by in a silent apology and went to turn the music off, the thought occurring to him that he should see if it was even Greg's CD.

He turned off the stereo with the end of his pen, then popped the CD case open. Bingo. Bloody fingerprint. Fuck, yes.

"Leah. Got a present for you."

Maybe. Just maybe they had something. Finally.

"Yeah?" Her eyes lit up, just dancing. "Oh, fucking A, Art. You get a gold star."

She scribbled frantically in a notebook. Thank God for her and her ability to focus on the details.

He let her have it, moving on, methodically checking shelves, up and down from center. There were books missing - he knew because Greg wouldn't stand for a surgical text to be beside a murder mystery. Pulling out his notebook and pen, Artie got to work, making notes. He could understand Leah. He really could.

"Leah? It's a bloodbath on the third floor." One of the crime scene boys was shaking his head. "That's where the messy work was done."

"You find the body?"

"Parts of it."

"Goddamn." Leah was gonna hurl again. "Whoever did this was here for hours, Artie. When did Greg leave last night?"

"It was at supper time. When I came and got him. Maybe six?" He thought. He had the pizza receipt somewhere.

"Okay, and the store closes at what? Seven? Opens at nine?" Leah chewed on her bottom lip. "He wouldn't have used the store... Amy? Honey? Go check the garbage cans outside at the base of the stairs."

"Yes, ma'am." Amy headed out.

"Books missing," Artie said. "Something here, too. Some kind of knick-knack."

"What kind? Looks like a box, maybe? Would Greg know if I asked?"

"Yeah. He doesn't keep much anymore. He'd know. I'll make a note." Greg knew everything, knew the history of it.

"'Kay." They kept moving. The bed was the hardest, white sheets stained and bloody, the crime unit cutting a square from the mattress.

Greg might not ever be able to come back here. It was going to break his heart. Artie sighed, checking the closet, his eye better than someone who didn't know Greg at all. It looked normal, line after line of not-dyed, not-synthetic, soft things. Greg's things. Still with his pen, noting that he needed to get gloves from someone's kit, Artie sorted through, just looking, frowning, making sure nothing was weird.

"Art? You find anything in there? Those reporters are getting into the building across the way, shooting film."

"I got nothing here. Can't we close shit off? Hang a blanket or something. I'll get Greg." He had to get Greg off the roof before someone got hurt.

"Okay. The guys didn't find any evidence the perp was in the store, Art. Maybe we can get him into his office? He can be alone in there."

"Yeah. I think I can do that. I'll go." Trudging, feeling old, Artie made his way up the stairs again, poking his head out. "Greg? Babe? They're gonna be taking your picture. They've cleared the shop. Can you manage the office?"

Those dark eyes met his from where Greg was sitting, hiding by the storage room. "I suppose. I can't stay here forever."

"No. No, you can't. Come on, man. We can get you settled. I'm not doing any good in there. I can...I can take your statement or something." God, he needed to get his shit together.

"Okay." Greg reached up for him, eyes sort of... sympathetic. "Will you take me home with you, after all this?"

Artie grinned back, finally feeling like he knew an answer. "Babe, I'd take you home right now if I didn't have all this work I had to do." He let his hand close around Greg's, let himself feel a moment. "That's not gonna change."

"Good." Greg stood up, looking pale, but *there*. "Okay. You open the door."

"Yeah." He let go of Greg to do it, not wanting to act like any kind of transmitter.

Greg walked - so careful, not touching, not leaning, not even seeming to breathe as they headed down the stairs. They got to the apartment and Greg swayed, eyes closing. Artie hurried him into the elevator, needing to get the man safe again. Well, safer.

"I don't know what I'll do, about here. I don't know if I can..." Greg shook his head, eyes staring at all the *people*, at the mess. "Artie? Who took my kit?"

"Your kit?"

"Yes. My surgeon's kit. It was a little rolled bag with a scalpel, forceps. They were my great-grandfather's. They're gone."

"I'll check. Come on. Down. We'll get you settled." Then he'd come back and hope to God there was someone to ream for moving the kit.

"Okay." Greg waited for him to open the elevator, wincing as people moved things, touched things. "Artie. Artie, can we bring your chair? Please? Before it's ruined."

"You bet. I'll bet it's clear." He left Greg standing there to go stop some poor pimple-faced kid just in time. "Don't touch, man. Let me clear it. Greg wants to take it downstairs to sit in."

"Sure, detective. Hands off."

The look on Greg's face made things... more solid. More like he could keep his feet under him. Of course, with that stability came the first flushes of hot anger. Artie lifted cushions and turned the chair up on its front legs, checking for weird stains or odd bumps in the upholstery, just in case. It looked okay, so he dragged it to the elevator.

Greg helped, entire body relaxing after his hands landed on the upholstery. "Just us. Thank God. Just you and me."

"Good. Let's get it out of here, then." Someplace Greg could curl up and relax downstairs would help. An oasis of calm. Artie wrestled it in and closed the gate, pushing the button for the ground floor.

"Is Alice okay? Mitch?" Greg just kept stroking the chair, eyes closed.

"Alice's a little shook up. Mitch came to get her. Leah's gonna check in on them later, and I put a uniform on their house on the Q.T." Just in case.

"Okay. You're a good cop, Artie. This isn't about you."

"I know. I'm not trying to. Shit. It's not me I'm worried about, Greg. I'm furious for you. And worried." And just. Feeling like it was personal, damn it.

"That's not what I meant. I mean... I mean it isn't your fault." Greg caught his eyes, just so fucking pale. "And I'm glad you're pissed. I'm pissed. That was my house."

"It still is. And it's fucking wrong." He reached out, put his hand on Greg's. "I'm sorry, babe."

"Yeah." Greg nodded, starting to shake a little, holding on to him. "Can we make coffee in the office?"

"We can. We'll put sugar in it." That would help with the shock. Artie moved around and held on, letting his arms close around Greg's waist.

Greg took a hitching breath, leaning fully into him. "Thank you."

"You're welcome, babe. We'll figure it out. I promise." They'd find this creep and they'd put him in jail until the end of the world.

"Yes. Do you think this is my fault?"

"No. I think this is the product of one deranged fucking mind. You just happen to be the target." No way could Greg be the thing that cracked this guy. He was just the thing that set the guy off this time. If not Greg, it would have been someone else.

Greg nodded. "Okay. Okay. Let's make coffee and I'll do the statement thing."

"Okay, babe." It seemed like they'd done this before. Several times. "Let's do it."

Artie got the chair settled, helped Greg make coffee, and sat down with his notebook and his pen.

He only hoped this was the last time he had to do this.

Chapter Eleven

It was almost nine before they pulled up to Artie's place, Artie's chair strapped in the trunk of the car.

Greg had stopped thinking hours ago. Stopped talking before that. Hell, he'd made three pots of coffee himself, drinking it hot and sweet, pouring it into himself as he curled in Artie's chair.

Artie swore no one had touched his clothes, so he had a bag of his own stuff packed and then a new hairbrush and toothbrush.

He wasn't sure what had been in the bathroom.

He didn't want to know.

They got the chair into the apartment, Duke mewling and spitting and worrying, jumping right on his suitcase and rubbing on it furiously.

"Thank you, Duke." Yeah, make it right again.

Artie chuckled, the first sound he'd made since they started the drive over, and it sounded like two rocks grinding together. "That damned cat always knows. Albacore for you tonight, buddy. Or smoked salmon."

Greg nodded, pushed Artie's chair to an out-of-the-way place and sat, curling into it with a sigh.

Artie puttered a little, feeding Duke, moving Greg's suitcase into the bedroom, taking off his coat and tie. Washing up a little. Then Artie just

came right to him and sat on the arm of the chair,
hand on his.

"Hey." If he closed his eyes, he could almost
pretend he was home.

"Hey." Artie didn't say anything else, really,
just stroked his hand, thumb moving on his skin.
Just touching.

He wasn't sure what it meant, that Artie's mind
was quiet, still.

Resting.

"You hungry?" Artie finally asked, as Duke
wandered over to rub around his feet.

"I should be, I suppose." No meat. He didn't
think he could face meat.

"I have some cereal. Some blueberries, I think."
Artie leaned a little more, heavy and warm, just
starting to melt into him a little.

"Mmmhmm." He nodded, shifted so Artie could
settle closer.

"We'll do that, then." Big as the man was, Artie
still managed to fit in the chair with him, slipping
down and half pulling him on those solid thighs.

He kept his eyes closed, fingers settling against
Artie's chest. He could feel Duke, right at his
ankles, purring and vibrating.

"Mmmm." Artie hummed, held on, those arms
around him, one hand on his back. They breathed
together, Artie's chest rising and falling
hypnotically.

Okay, he could just stay.

Right here.

Greg dozed, waking himself up every time he
slipped deep enough to dream.

Artie was there every time, petting him,
murmuring, "I got you, babe. Right here."

"Right here." God, he was tired, bone-deep weary.

"Yep. With me." Artie's lips grazed his forehead, those hands starting to dig into his muscles, easing the aches.

"Oh..." The sound that left him sounded almost broken. Almost, damn it.

"Yeah. Yeah, it's okay, Greg. Whatever you need." So good to him. So good. Artie sat, loved on him, mumbled nonsense words.

"It feels good. Nothing ought to feel good right now."

Nothing should feel anything but raw.

"Why not? We gotta rest sometime." That poor voice. Artie sounded so hoarse. So tired. As tired as he felt.

"Yeah. Yeah, I could rest for a while." A month. A year.

"Me, too, babe. We should go to like, Fiji. Hell, I'd settle for the Outer Banks." He could feel the tiny smile that curved Artie's mouth. He nodded, kept his eyes closed as a dull, horrified panic rushed over him again. Someone -- a killer -- had been in his house. He hadn't been farther than Artie's apartment in almost a decade.

Artie's hands soothed him, smoothing out the tension in his muscles as he tensed up. "Shh. I got you. I got you."

"Got me. I'm sorry. It's just--" He took a deep breath, tried to relax. "It's been a long day."

"No. No apologies. I just want you to try to relax, babe. I know it's hard."

"What am I going to do? I don't... I." Greg looked up at Artie, heart just pounding. "Last night

was the first night I'd spent away from home since
I came here."

Artie stared right back at him, serious as a heart
attack. "We'll find you a safe place, Greg. Some
place you love. I promise." The look turned to a
funny little grimace. "For right now my place will
have to do."

He frowned, fingers reaching for Artie, needing
to know what that look meant, what Artie meant.
Artie took his hand, rubbed it against that stubbly
cheek. Artie was worried that his place wasn't good
enough, that it was too messy, too much Duke, not
safe enough. Worried that Greg wasn't going to
want to stay.

"I--" He tugged Artie closer, brought their lips
together. "There isn't too much Duke, too much
you."

"Oh, good." Artie kissed him, lips pushing
against his, tongue opening his mouth, suddenly
urgent instead of soothing.

Greg gasped, let the hunger push him along a
little, let it push away at the fear and fury. It
pushed everything out in front of it, Artie cupping
the back of his head and kissing him hard, bruising
his mouth a little, his lips swelling.

More. More. He arched, demanding, entire
body taut.

Artie cupped his butt and pulled, giving him
leverage, something to push against as Artie moved
under him, surrounded him. The kiss got toothy,
Artie groaning for him. He just let it take him, let
all the shit and worry go and just rocked, took all
the pleasure Artie offered him. And Artie offered a
lot, tugging at his shirt, his soft pants, getting him
naked so those rough hands could move over his

skin, could find all of his hot spots. The underside of his arms, the back of his neck, his lower belly...Artie touched them all, teased them.

Those hands. God. Greg did his best to touch back, to return the favor, but he was caught in everything Artie was giving him. That was okay. He could feel Artie's need to give, to make it better. Could hear the man thinking like he was saying it out loud. Artie wanted this for him. One hand dropped to Greg's lap, stroking his cock, making him crazy.

His head fell back, hips snapping up into that touch. That hand. "Artie..."

"Uh-huh. Greg. Babe." That voice still sounded blown, but now it was sexy rough. Hot.

"Yeah. Yeah, I need." He did. He needed this, just as much as Artie did. Greg forced his eyes open, forced himself to focus, to see Artie, right there.

"Me, too, babe." He could see the grimace now, one of utter pleasure, the worry and stress of the day gone for that moment.

"I feel you." He laughed, caught right there. "I feel you. Christ."

"Yeah. I need. Babe. My pants." Artie shivered beneath him, hand still working him, hips rolling.

Okay. Pants. Right. He got his hands down there, working Artie's zipper down.

"Oh." Artie panted for him, thick cock pushing right up into his hand as he got through the pants and underwear. Hot and wet, Artie felt so good, took the rest of the bad thoughts right out of his head.

"Yeah. Yeah, want." He wanted Artie everywhere. Anywhere. But now this was right. Desperate. Heated. Now.

Hauling him up even more, Artie got them where their cocks pressed together, where he could get friction. They both moaned at the feel of it.

Oh, yeah. Just. That was. God. Greg kissed Artie hard, panting and groaning into those lips.

They rocked, the chair creaking but holding, their skin heating almost unbearably. Artie groaned for him, not making sense, but he didn't have to. Greg could hear him through their skin.

Want. Hot. Good. Love. He could hear it. Love.

His hips snapped, heat shooting out of him and leaving him vibrating. Artie humped up, body going tight as a wire, cock jerking in Greg's hand as he came, too, nothing in his thoughts but pure pleasure, pure need for Greg. Pure love.

That was what he needed. Just that. Just right now.

"Thank you." His cheek rested on Artie's shoulder.

"Mmmhmm. Better." Artie just leaned against him, too, heavy and solid. Breathing him in.

"Uh-huh." He just nodded. Felt.

Artie stroked his back, soothing, just making them both slow down, calm down. "You'll stay, yeah? For a while?"

"With you? Until you get tired of me."

Those heavy arms wrapped around him again, holding him, making him feel safe even if just for a little bit. "Then you're gonna be here a while," Artie said, squeezing.

And Greg could feel the truth of it, all the way to his bones.

"Good thing we have your chair." He smiled, foot carefully petting Duke, just sliding.

"Uh-huh. It's a good chair." Comfy. Sturdy. Like Artie.

"It is." He listened to Artie's stomach rumble, growl. Someone was hungry.

"I could make some eggs or something," Artie said, just like he'd heard Greg's thoughts. "Toast. Or maybe some veggie soup. I have some canned minestrone."

"Cereal is good. Then we'll make something better after we shower."

"Okay. We could both stand some steam." Artie didn't sound inclined to move, but his stomach growled again, and they both chuckled.

Greg thought it was one of the best sounds he'd ever heard. Them. Laughing. Together.

Artie agreed, from the sound of it, hugging him tight and kissing him hard. "Corn flakes or Cocoa Puffs?"

"Ooh. Cocoa Puffs. You get chocolate milk at the end."

"Uh-huh. Duke loves it." Duke purred at that, leaping up on their legs, claws carefully sheathed.

"He's a cat of exquisite taste." He stroked Duke's head and ears, loving that happy rumble.

"He is. He loves you." Artie's hand covered his, helping pet and stroke Duke's silky smooth coat. Greg heard the echo of Artie's, "Like me," through the touch.

Greg nodded. Yes. Yes, he knew that. Bone-deep.

Chapter Twelve

The phone was ringing as Artie struggled with
the grocery bags and the door, Duke yowling like a
feline demon on the other side. Damn it, where the
hell was Greg? He could answer the phone, or get
the door or... A bag slipped and suddenly Artie had
a milk bomb, white liquid flying all over the hall.

The door opened, Greg in a pair of shorts, scrub
brush in one hand. Jesus Christ. It must only be
fifty degrees inside. All the window were open, all
the lights were on, and Greg was cleaning.

Again.

Duke shot out like a streak and started licking
the walls. Oh, ew. "Duke, no." Artie nudged the
big cat with his toes.

"Sorry." Greg opened the door and stepped back
to let him in, scooping Duke up before the damned
cat tore his toes off.

"No problem, babe. The walls needed a milk
bath. Would you do me a favor and wipe that down
while I put this stuff away and shut the windows?"
He still had three bags.

"Sure." Greg crouched in the hall, muscles
clenching and relaxing as he scrubbed.

That made the day better, it surely did. Artie
plopped the groceries down and opened a bag of

salmon, knowing Duke would come running. Keep the damned cat out of the hall.

Duke yowled, purring and moaning and rubbing up against him. O, ye fickle feline.

"I'd rather it was Greg doing that," Artie mumbled, putting away a six-pack of beer and a bottle of some kind of...macrobiotic yogurt. There was a bit of tofu cheese stuff and some organic gray crap in there. Alice must have been by.

"Greg? What the hell is this gray shit?" Artie called, hoping it was Alice and not something growing hair, because Greg would have a fit.

"Uh... Some kinda hummus, I think. It tastes better than it smells."

"It had better taste better than it looks." God, it looked like crap. But then Greg probably thought his olive loaf was frightening.

"That is, unfortunately, open to interpretation." Greg leaned against the look-through, almost smiling. "Did you get anything horribly decadent?"

"I did. I got us one of those brownie mixes with the little baggies of caramel and fudge that you pour in." He'd found that Greg did better with stuff that Artie had to mix and cook than he did with ready made cakes and stuff.

"Oh, mmm." He got a grin that he knew meant Greg appreciated it, knew he was trying.

"So you have any trouble today?" He asked it casually, but he needed to know.

"I... I tried to go to the store with Alice. I didn't get far." Greg shrugged, looking a little sheepish. "So I came back."

"That's okay. You tried." Greg had never gotten out well. Since he'd lost most of his stuff...well. It had been hard.

"Yeah. Did you find anything out? Anyone walk in and confess?"

"No." He chuckled. That would be nice, wouldn't it? "We've been passing the tape from my desk around. The fingerprint is in the lab. The inventory at your place is almost done."

"What does that mean? I can go back? Can put it on the market, if I want to?"

"I haven't asked, babe. I just know they're almost done with the whole deal, according to Leah." Leah was a champ, handling shit Artie just couldn't, and not even bitching about him getting too emotionally involved.

"Oh. Okay." Greg nodded, starting to wander a little again, still a little lost, a little at sea.

"Come here?" He grinned as Greg looked over, and Artie held out a hand, wanting to touch. That was a little awkward still, too, knowing he never knew how Greg would react to it.

That got him another smile, though, and Greg came right over, fingers twining with his. "Hey."

Artie held on, letting the touch ease the tension of the day. "Hey. Damn, you feel good."

"Better and better." Greg's eyes closed, muscles bunching and then relaxing. Gently, slowly, so Greg could break away if need be, Artie pulled Greg in, letting that skinny body rest against his. "Oh. Oh, you feel." Greg got a little rambly as he picked up God knew what. "Do not. Just. You feel good."

Sometimes he wondered where that psychic antenna went, because on the surface Artie figured his thoughts said nothing to argue about. Grinning a little, he sorta rocked, just enjoying. Greg chuckled, chin snuggling right into the hollow of his collarbone.

"So. What do you want for supper, besides brownies?" They'd eaten a lot of eggs. That was okay, it was normal. But he could do other stuff. Not gray hummus.

"Pasta? I like pasta. Or just salmon and cream cheese on crackers."

"Oh, we could have pasta. I can do that." He could. He even knew how to make this fresh tomato and basil thing. The salmon would be gone by now, if Duke was true to form.

"Good. I'll help." Greg didn't move, though, just stayed there for another long minute. "I'm going to sell Alice and Mitch the store. They want it."

Artie leaned back to look at him. "Okay. We can talk about it." Sure. Right. That made him blink a little, but they had time to see what Greg really wanted to do.

Greg's head tilted, face suddenly worried. "I'm not suggesting that I'd live off you or anything of the sort, Artie. I wouldn't."

"No. I know that." He grinned a little. Dork. "I just don't want you to rush it. You know. Stuff."

"Yeah. I just. Everything is..." Greg sighed, met his eyes. "Everything is so different."

"I know." His hands felt overlarge and clumsy as he patted Greg's back, letting go afterwards so he could go start pasta water. "I do know, babe."

Greg went to the refrigerator, rummaging and finding chopped garlic, tomatoes, butter.

They puttered together for a while, the silence easier now, both of them more relaxed. Even if they did have to work around Duke, who sprawled

in a feline nap attack on the counter, belly
distended with salmon.

He got a glass of wine to sip as he cooked, Greg
cutting the bread, humming along with whatever
song was in the man's head. There was that antenna
again. Artie turned the heat on under the tomatoes
as the water boiled and he dropped a couple of
handfuls of pasta in. It was...well, under different
circumstances it would have been homey. Good. It
was, really, but the reason was always there.

It figured, didn't it, that they'd get together
under the shadow of some weird-assed serial killer.
It almost made sense, in a backassward sort of
way.

He added mushrooms and salt and some basil,
watching tomatoes split and bubble. Yeah. It
figured. "Oh, the bread smells good," he said, just
then realizing it had gone into the oven.

"Thank you." Greg stopped suddenly, looked
over at him. "Do you have a backgammon board,
Artie?"

"Uh." Did he? Shit. "If I do it's in the cabinet by
the couch. The pine thing."

"Okay. I'll look." Greg disappeared, Duke
actually lifting his head and watching before
slumping back down on the counter.

Artie tried not to watch or twitch. Who knew
what was in that cabinet. Or what Greg would get
off of it. He heard the cabinet open, heard a brief
rattle, and then it closed again, his chair creaking
as Greg settled in it.

His chair. It made him smile how much Greg
loved that chair. How safe he felt in it. Shit.
Spitting tomatoes. Duke was spitting, too, flying
up.

"Do you need any help, detective? Duke looks... fluffy and vaguely pissed."

"I had a tomato burst." He laughed, moving shit around and turning off burners. The pasta timer went off, and he drained it, moving automatically.

Greg wandered back in and rescued the bread, hip just bumping against him. He grinned, then made sure everything was off before grabbing Greg and kissing him silly, needing the contact. He'd have to remember to do that more often, considering the way Greg moaned and went boneless, really relaxing.

The kissing went on, but that was okay. Dinner was good reheated. Really. Greg chuckled into the kisses, hands stroking over his face, down his throat. Uh-huh. Oh, yeah. An appetizer. Artie traced the planes of Greg's body, feeling too many ribs.

Greg stretched under his touch, arching almost like Duke would. The thought made him smile again. He liked the smiling. That part was good. He liked the touching, too. This kind. Any kind as long as it came from Greg. Greg hummed a little, nibbled on his bottom lip. It stunned him, that this sensual man had spent years not being touched. Not at all. Stunned him, made him all growly on Greg's behalf, and yet a selfish little part of him was glad that *he* was the one who could do it and get away with it.

And didn't Greg let him see how good it was? They settled against the counter, Greg's hands cupping his balls, rolling them nice and easy. Artie grunted, body zinging like he'd touched a live wire. He humped into Greg's hand, his own hands pulling them closer together. Yeah. That was. Yeah.

"Mmmhmm." Greg nodded, agreeing to God knew what. Those fingers pushed harder, finding one hot spot after another. Lord.

He touched Greg, counting down Greg's spine, fingers slipping down to stroke the crease of Greg's ass. The things this man made him want...

"Mmm? Tell me." Greg nuzzled, licked at his jaw.

"Want you. All over. Here on the counter. On the floor on your knees. Want inside you. Want to suck you." He'd be embarrassed with anyone else, but this was Greg. Why be worried when the man could see it anyway?

"Artie. Yes. God." Oh, Greg liked that, jerked against him and sorta started humping.

He lifted Greg a little, turning so that thin body was pressed against the counter all the way, giving them leverage as he humped right back, moaning. Yeah. He couldn't really even think anymore. He'd do all those things soon, though.

"Uh-huh. Soon. Artie." Greg's fingers scraped all up his spine, pulling him in tight.

"Yeah. Greg. Babe. I...wow." His head snapped back, his whole body arching as he came, just like that. Boom. Greg shook, holding off and just riding it with him, eyes big as anything, staring at him like he was pure magic.

"Babe. Come on." Now he could watch, could see Greg's face, and he pressed Greg into his thigh, really gave the man something to rub on.

"Yes." Greg's face went flushed, dark eyes rolling like dice as all the tension and shit got shoved aside and Greg just felt. It took one thrust, maybe two or three, and yeah, yeah, good. Greg came for him, and Artie watched it, watched every flicker of expression on Greg's face.

God, blissed out looked good on his man. Fucking hot. Artie grinned and kissed and loved on Greg a little. The man deserved it.

"Feels so good." Greg's head rolled on his shoulders a little, eyes dazed.

"Uh-huh. Wanna sit? I'll get supper re-heated." He got them cleaned up, then guided Greg to his chair, the walk from the kitchen seeming long. A trudge.

"Mmmhmm..." Greg snagged the garlic bread on the way, fed him a bite as they walked.

"Yum. Okay, be back with salad and shit." There was, uh. Pasta. Yeah. And bread. Oh, that was good bread.

"Yeah." Greg was purring, almost as loud as Duke.

Artie laughed and went to get the food, Duke appearing as if Artie thinking about him had brought him running. You'd think the silly cat hadn't just eaten a whole bag of salmon the way he was carrying on.

There was something fine about the sound of Greg's voice, soft and rumbling, calling Duke right over. They had supper, both of them yawning like crazy, both of them starting to blink and drift. Looked like no TV for them tonight.

"Mmm. Wanna take a movie into the bedroom? Something easy." Greg leaned over, shoulder against him, the action natural and easy.

"Sure. Something we can sleep to." He knew that much. He dumped the dishes in the sink to soak and they moved on to the bedroom, more into the cuddling than the watching.

Greg settled right into the curve of his body, cheek on his upper arm, fingers twined with his. Artie settled in and let himself really relax, letting their breathing coordinate. It was good to have Greg in his bed, no matter what the circumstances.

Real good.

Chapter Thirteen

"Greg? Honey? You okay?"

Greg stared over at Alice, trying his best to nod. "I think so?"

He'd made it here. Finally. After ten days. It almost felt good, wandering through his store, seeing the books, the stones and statues and odd little knick-knacks. The life he'd created for himself after the move.

"Well, it's good to see you here..."

"Yeah. It was a good, long walk. Winter's coming."

"Christmas, yeah? You going to put up your tree with the organ ornaments?" Alice's eyes flew open and her mouth made an "o." "Oh, lord and lady. Greg. Honey, I'm. Oh. Oh, that was..."

Greg blinked a second and started laughing, deep and hard, all the tired muscles from his walk protesting, but his heart just tickled as hell. Alice started laughing with him, plopping down on the stool behind the register. God, if anyone came in right now they'd think both of them were drunk or crazed. Possibly both.

Speak of the devil, the little bell over the door rang, and in came Artie, looking at them both with this wide-eyed stare, tie almost up under one ear.

Alice smiled over at Artie, the look a little odd and knowing. "Thought you'd lost him, huh?"

"Huh? Well, he coulda asked for a ride." Now the look was sheepish, Artie's square face just showing everything he was thinking. At least to Greg, anyway.

"I walked." He figured that would go over like a lead balloon, but he'd needed out and couldn't face Alice's car.

"Do you have any idea..." Artie took a deep breath, stopping whatever he was about to say and just standing there, looking a little lost.

"I think I'm going to go, Greg honey. Artie, you take care." Alice stood and grinned. "Greg, leave the deposit locked in the office if you can't handle the cash."

"It's not like we're going to fight, Alice."

"Why should things be different now than ever, honey? You two go after it better than anyone." Little bitch.

Artie's eyes snapped up, and, oh, he gave Alice an evil look. "See you later, Alice."

"Night, detective." She grabbed her purse, almost bouncing, almost laughing out loud.

They both watched her go before Artie threw the lock and turned back to him, a huge breath swelling that square chest. "What the *fuck* were you thinking?"

Greg blinked, one eyebrow arching up to his hairline. "Excuse me? I was thinking I needed to get to work."

"But walking? Christ, Greg." The tie hit the floor, Artie doing a complicated dance to get it off, stomping it with one foot. "You could have been snatched."

"What did that tie ever do to you?" Snatched. Right. He knew. Sort of.

"I fucking hate ties. Goddamned little nooses of death." Artie kicked the tie, that "so there" expression so comical it hurt.

"You've lost your mind. Leah finally cracked and slipped something in that sludge you call coffee."

"Maybe I have! Goddamn it, Greg. I worry about you. My cat is more psycho every day because I'm fucking you and he's not, or something. Leah is in pregnant woman mode. And there's a killer on the loose, in case you forgot."

"Duke doesn't mind the fucking part. He just doesn't like the brand of tuna you picked up on sale." Like he could fucking forget. Like he could ever forget.

"Oh, fuck that." Sighing, Artie rolled his neck. "So you walked. Everything went okay. So I'll get over it."

"Okay." He nodded, moved over toward the register. He almost missed fighting with Artie. Playing.

"No. You know what? It's not okay." He got intercepted midway, Artie grabbing him and shaking him like a mongoose with a snake. "Don't do that, babe. Just don't."

Wave after wave of shit hit him, but he pushed it away, growling right back. "I'm a fucking grown up. I needed to come to work, sign checks."

"Well, whoopdeedoo," Artie said, that pure North Carolina accent going deep. "I need to know you're safe. Not only is it my job, it's damned fucking important to me."

"What am I supposed to do? Wait for him to find where I am? Wait for him to find you? Hell, he wants to fuck up my life, he wants my attention, not *me*!"

"What if he changes his pattern?" Artie shook him again, boom, back and forth. "Jesus fuck."

"What if he does? I'm not a little blonde girl. Let him come in, damn it. He's a fucking coward, thinking he can steal my life!" The sudden fury surprised him, shocked him.

Those eyes widened, and he could feel Artie's surge of fear for him mingled with admiration. "I need you, Greg."

"I'm not going anywhere, Artie." He met Artie's eyes. "This. Us. It's not about him."

Not about that fucking bastard.

"No. It never has been." Oh, God, that look in those eyes. It was all heat and need and raw, all of it right there.

"No." Greg pushed right up against Artie, their chests slapping together audibly and, fuck. It was hot.

Artie groaned and pulled him closer still, hands hard on him with something more than anger. That mouth. God, Artie had a fine mouth. God, they spent so long walking on fucking eggshells that he'd forgotten that it could be so hot. They smacked up against...something. The counter. Something, Artie so desperate against him, so rough. Like the dam had broken.

"More." He didn't want Artie to think, to stop. Not now.

"Definitely." Nope. That wasn't thinking. Not at all. Not when Artie was biting his throat that way. He was caught in it, trapped in the passion, the heat. In Artie. His head fell back, throat working as he let Artie have more.

"Mmmhmm." That was the deep, low growl of a man who wanted, and Artie gave him that and everything else, teeth stinging his skin.

He worked Artie's shirt open, nails sliding down Artie's chest, enough to make the man feel it.

"Uhn." Yeah, Artie felt it. Greg knew by the shiver that ran through those big muscles, by the way Artie bucked against him. "Need you."

"Right here." Belt next. Shirt, then pants.

His own clothes started to sorta...disappear, Artie yanking at them like he had that ridiculous tie earlier. Then they were at least mostly naked and rubbing, Artie bruising him with the power of it.

Artie got him up on the counter a little, legs spread enough to wrap around Artie's hips and start rubbing like it was nobody's business. They rocked, Artie grunting, jockeying for better position. Then they hit the perfect spot and just went with it, the friction sending sizzling heat up his spine.

"I. Good. Good, Artie." He leaned down, mouth fastening on the join of Artie's shoulder and neck, sucking and licking.

"Shit! Greg." Cock poking him, Artie rubbed and pushed, skin starting to slick up under Greg's hands and mouth. "Again."

"Yeah." Oh, hell, yeah. That was what he needed, passion. Heat. Need. Right now. He bit down, teeth scratching along Artie's skin.

"God..." He felt Artie's wetness against his belly, felt that thick prick jerk against him as Artie cried out, body heaving. "Greg. You. I."

"Uh-huh." He nodded, riding it out, just lost in Artie, in the salt and soap and smoke flavor.

Then Artie's hand closed around him, pulling, demanding he give it all up, kissing him so hard he tasted blood. Everything in him went tight and hard and hot, and he growled out Artie's name as he shot, ass sliding on the counter.

"Yeah. Yeah, like that." So much better than that fucking tie, Artie was thinking, so much happier now.

He started chuckling, nodding against Artie's shoulder. Okay, so. Ties. Bad. Right. "Good. Hey."

"Hey." Artie sighed, leaned against him. "Hey."

"Not going to apologize." He'd walk more if it got him fucked like that.

"Fuckhead." It had no heat behind it but it still made him laugh, the way it sounded like something Artie thought was just a bad, bad word.

"Yeah, yeah, yeah. Bad-ass detective." He couldn't stop grinning, leaning in and resting.

Artie's chest vibrated under him, chuckles sounding happy and deep.

God, that was something else. Better than...

Well, okay.

Maybe not better.

Still, it was damned good.

"Better?" Artie asked, hands stroking up and down his back, stopping where his ass met the counter. Artie certainly sounded better, looser, much easier in his bones.

"Yeah. Getting rid of the tie was a good idea."

"I think it's tamed." He got a pinch for his trouble, Artie laughing as both of their stomachs growled at the same time.

"There's only Alice's stuff down here." Artie had this unreasoning prejudice against macrobiotic food. "You want to go home and order pizza?"

"Sure. Long as you let me drive." Artie grunted for him as he pinched this time. "Oof."

"Chicken. I used to drive." Years ago.

"You think you're up to it now?" There was that underlying edge of seriousness, Artie lifting up to look at him. "I meant no more walking, though."

"You worry too much." He stroked Artie's nose. There was no way he could drive. No way he could trust himself.

"I know. I'd apologize, but it wouldn't help." There. That was the gruff, blunt Artie he knew and loved.

"I know. We'll figure it out." His eyes shot to the elevator, the urge to go upstairs sudden and strong.

"Only if you want to. They've cleared it. But I'm not letting you scrub." Artie knew him too damned well. Knew him well enough that the man didn't need talents like his to read him.

"I don't want to. No, I want to, but not now. Now I want to go home with you and feed Duke." He was altogether too fond of that tom.

"Okay. We'll get the extra meat pizza for him." That was no joke. Duke could eat a whole medium with spicy sausage.

"And those apple puff pastry things." He nodded, grinning suddenly as he realized there were going to be ass prints on the counter.

"What are you laughing at, buddy? My need for flaky crust?"

"Nope. My need for Pledge before Alice kills us."

Artie blinked at him, then looked down at the counter and started laughing, the sound booming, almost startling. Artie grabbed his thighs and bent double, laughing so hard he wheezed.

Oh, hell. He started chuckling, hand landing on the small of Artie's back. "I...I'm never going to touch that counter again without getting hard."

"Oh, good. I can just see it now, Alice staring at your pants." Poor Artie was going to choke to death, he just knew it.

"Ew! Ew, Alice's like... a mom or a sister or something. EW!" Oh, God. Greg loved that man.

"Yeah, yeah. Sisters look. You don't have to think of them that way, but if you're wandering about with a hard-on..." Artie cupped his cock, nothing urgent or anything, just gentle, hot.

"Bastard." He chuckled, shook his head a little. They'd laughed more in the last half hour than they had in days.

"Uh-huh. Just a big old meanie." The lines around Artie's eyes had evened out, become the smile lines they should be, and those wide shoulders looked less tense, more normal.

"Yeah. I think I should keep you." In fact, he might have to keep Artie a long, long while.

Chapter Fourteen

"'Lo?" Artie blinked blearily at the clock. He'd worked all night on a new case and his ass was dragging. It was like...ten A.M. Shit. Was he supposed to be at work?

"Artie. I got the fucker. I got him." Leah sounded frantic, whispering into the phone. "It's the fucking electrician."

"What?" He levered up on one elbow, trying to shake off the sleep. "Who what?"

"Bruckle. Fucking Andy Bruckle. The electrician. The one in the videotape. I spent the night following him; he has a white Ford pickup, just like the doc said. I did some calling, and the guy used to be Jerry Daniels, went to school up at USC while Greg was teaching. Applied to be Greg's TA three months before Greg's accident and got turned down."

"No shit?" He fumbled, his hand automatically searching for Greg. "Where are you? What's he up to?"

"I'm at the guy's apartment, man. I got Judge Harris to sign a search warrant. He headed off about ten minutes ago, and Baker and Williams are shadowing him."

"Oh, good. You be careful, you hear?" God knew he didn't need anything to happen to Leah. "I'll come."

"Yeah, yeah. You get Greg to tell you about him, man. See what he remembers. God, you should see this place, Art. It's all fucking books. Everywhere. Like a library."

"Look for Greg's book. We need something to tie. You know?" Where the fuck was Greg? Artie finally got untangled, got out of bed, looking. He heard the shower running, Duke yowling at the bathroom door, insisting that Greg shouldn't be in there getting wet. Oh. Good. For a minute there his heart had tried to do things it shouldn't with the pounding. "I'll get Greg on it. What else?"

"I don't know. We need to figure if we're going to take him in now or see if he's got another one somewhere, yeah? They can't be here. There's no room."

"Shit. Okay. We may have to wait. There's nowhere to go underground there?" He patted his chest where his pocket would be if he had one, kinda blushing when he realized he was naked on the phone with Leah.

"Not that I see. This is a third story place."

"Shit," he said again, searching for...pants. Something like pants. "Okay, then we need to see what he might own. I take it he rents there?"

"Yeah. He's been here at this place eighteen months. Bruckle moved to Raleigh seven months after the Doc did. Working as a subcontractor - first the community college, then Greg's building, the dry cleaner's next door. That little deli. The police station."

"Goddamn, he's got us coming and going. Bastard." They were gonna get him now, though. Artie knew it.

"Yeah. I just can't figure what the deal is with the girls, if it's about Greg. I mean, shit, Greg was out of the closet back then."

"It has to be something he thinks is wrapped up in Greg, but is his own deal." Psychos were psychos. Who knew what they thought?

"I guess. I..." Her voice stopped short. "Fuck. Someone's opening the door."

"Leah! Get the hell out of there. Go." Oh, Jesus. Artie started hunting his shoes, frantic now.

He heard the phone clatter to the ground. "Hold it right there! Police! Freeze!"

Fuck, fuck, fuck. Fuck. He had to. Shit. Artie grabbed his gun, his jacket, fumbling for Greg's phone so he could keep his line open for Leah. "Dispatch. I need the address Detective Morales is searching. Now!"

"Artie? What's wrong?"

"Goddamnit! I said freeze! Put the fucking thing down, man!"

"I need your identification, sir."

He shoved a hand back at Greg, the whole three voices thing too much as he found his pen and barked his badge number into the phone. Come on, come on.

"6125-C Maple; off Hemlock."

Shots sounded in his left ear, Leah's scream sudden and sharp.

Artie all but sobbed, barking, "Officer needs backup at that location, shots fired," before dropping Greg's phone and running, the address still wet on his hand. Car keys. Fuck. There. He hit the stairs, his phone still pressed to his ear. "Hang in there, partner."

There was a click, a snap as the phone was picked up off the ground. "Detective."

A thousand things ran through his mind, threats, curses, but Artie went into cop mode. Finally. His voice stayed rock steady as he spoke. "What do you want? If you've killed a cop..."

"I haven't killed anyone, detective. I have perfected them. She's not terribly lovely, you know. Almost manlike..."

Leah. Jesus fuck. Artie tore the Camaro's door open, gunning the engine as soon as he could. "You don't want to hurt her. You really don't."

"No. No, she isn't my type at all, detective. However, I believe you and I are in a position to make a trade."

"I asked you what you wanted." Keep him talking, Artie. Keep him there. I'm coming, Leah.

"I want him. He has something I need."

"What? I can't help you unless you tell me why, man." He was gonna puke. He just knew it.

"Don't play games with me, detective. You know what he does. You know what he sees. I helped him find that. It belongs with me. It always has." He could hear the man moving, hear something sliding.

"What are you looking for? What is he gonna help you find, huh?" No, no moving. Surely a uniform was on the way, right? Surely.

"Perfection. I have to go, detective. I have things to do. I'll call you to arrange the switch, yes? I imagine you'll want to kiss him goodbye before you give him to me. Damaged goods, but he is a very unique case."

"Wait!" It came out of his mouth just before the line went dead and Artie growled, pushing more speed out of his Goddamned car.

He was never gonna get there in time. When he squealed to a stop, the place was crawling with uniforms, sirens and lights lighting the fucking day right up.

Artie stormed right through the crowd, flashing his badge, amazed he remembered it. "The cop. There was a cop here. Any sign of her?" He was barking and he knew it, but he couldn't stop himself.

"No, sir. There's a blood trail leading down the stairs, and we have a vehicle ID and witnesses, but..."

God fucking damn it.

"Well you get your asses out there and find her. You hear me? You find her." Leah was his partner. He'd do whatever he had to, no matter what, to get her back.

"Yes, sir." The uniforms scattered as he stormed upstairs, determined to find something, anything.

That was Leah's blood. The very thought gave him the cold sweats, thinking about her and her baby and her husband and what this was going to do to all of them. He took a deep breath through his nose, trying to hold on, to think. For her sake. Oh, fuck.

Greg.

Artie yanked out his phone and dialed Greg's cell.

"Artie?"

"Greg. Babe. Are you all right? Did you lock the door? Lock the door."

"Okay. Is she okay?" He heard Duke yowling up a storm, heard Greg locking the door, the chain rattling.

"No." Artie looked around, just letting his brain process what his eyes saw, not thinking too much. Sometimes that helped. "She found him, Greg. And now he has her."

"Oh, God."

The place was dark, dim, books stacked everywhere. Surgical texts. Biology texts. Books on dissection and photography and electrical engineering.

"I need to know everything you know about a Jerry Daniels, Greg. You turned him down once, for an assistantship." Dissection. Artie swallowed, making himself move past the fear.

"Who? I turned down a hundred people a year, Artie. I... Wait. I... He wasn't even an anatomy student, right? Electrical engineering."

"Yeah. Yeah, that's how he got into the station, how he got into your place..." Book, book, some kind of weird folder full of fuses.

"I... He was pissed, but no more than anyone. Sucked up. Came to the hospital after the fall. Why didn't I know it, Artie?"

"He said some shit, babe. We'll talk about it. I need to clear the scene now. I'll come get you soon, though. We're going to have to find you a safe place. He wants you."

"I want to see his house. I can find her, Artie. I'll be able to find her."

"I know. The place is crawling with uniforms. You'd short out. Give me an hour. Maybe two." Artie hoped to God Leah had that long. He'd bet she did. The guy needed her to at least make like he would do the exchange.

"Okay, Artie. I'll be here. She'll be fine."

"Love you." He needed to say it, even if it made the kid standing duty on the door stare. Artie hung up, hoping Greg was right. Hoping Leah would be just fine. She had to be.

***

If he was stuck in this apartment for any longer, Greg was going to have a psychotic break and wreak havoc with his faithful sidekick, Duke the one-eyed demon kitty, at his side.

He'd cleaned. Puked. Cleaned again. Unlocked the door a dozen times and each fucking time the phone rang.

It was surreal.

And deeply fucked.

And made him think that maybe Artie was having the apartment watched or filmed or something.

Of course, that led him into that weird paranoid space, which he wasn't going to entertain right now. Honestly. No. No, he was going to just stand up, walk to the door, open it and go find Maple.

If Artie hadn't been standing there when the door opened, it would have all worked much more effectively. "Well, hey there, babe."

God, Artie looked gray.

"Hey. Anything?" He stepped back, let Artie in.

"Not really, no. We know where he lives. We know his vehicle. We've got jack. Waiting for him to call." Artie sighed, rubbed the back of his neck, and even Duke didn't give him shit.

"What does he want?" He headed to make more coffee. Something.

"You. He wants to trade her for you. He says he can use you." Oh, Artie was *pissed* about that.

"Me." God. "Okay. Tell him to name a place and time."

"No!" Artie waved both hands wildly, looking like he wished he had a tie on. Greg had a sudden image of one flying out the window of the Camaro to be crushed in traffic. "No, I will not put you in danger like that."

"She's hurt. She's pregnant. She's your partner. I'm not a weakling. Maybe if you do it, he'll put himself in a spot you can grab him."

Hell, of all the ways he'd become worthless in the last ten years, maybe this was the way he made up for it.

"I know you're not." One hand scrubbing over his face, Artie turned and headed to the kitchen, grabbing a beer before speaking again. "It goes against all of my training to give in to demands, Greg. And to put a witness or victim at risk. For that person to be you..."

"Better me than Leah, Artie." They were created to reproduce, repopulate. It was a biological imperative.

The look on Artie's face was pure agony. "I don't wanna lose either one, babe."

"Well, I don't particularly want you to, either, but surely our priority is getting her medical attention, huh?" He headed over, hands sliding on Artie's shoulders.

Artie tensed up, shoulders like rock. "I. Yeah. Yeah, but, Greg..." The man was a giant swirl of emotion, most of it pitch-black.

"Breathe, detective." He stepped around behind Artie, knowing he couldn't keep the expressions off his face, the vague, sick horror.

Artie pivoted, hands reaching for him. "Quit that. Quit hiding. I'm sorry, I can't help what I'm thinking..."

"I know. You shouldn't have to. Worry, I mean. I just wanted to touch you." He'd gotten spoiled.

"Then come here." Artie pulled him close, and now he could feel the relief, the need. Artie was scared to death, but he made it better.

He nodded, tugged Artie closer, held on. This was all... "Was this all because I didn't give him an assistantship?"

"I don't know. He says you belong to him." A flash of hard anger, not at him, came through so clearly his ears rang. "You don't belong to anyone, babe." Artie paused, laughed. "Maybe Duke."

"You and Duke can share." Greg racked his brains, trying to remember the guy, remember something besides a few furious emails, a nasty letter.

"He has all this shit, Greg. Dissection texts. Weird philosophy books. It's like something out of a movie." Artie shook his head, nuzzling Greg's cheek.

"Take me over there? Maybe I can figure out where he goes. That's where he'll take her, right? To his lair?" Lair? What a comic book kind of word.

"Are you sure? I don't want you to overload, babe." The grooves around Artie's mouth made him sure.

"I'm sure. I want to help." He wanted to do something.

"Okay. We'll go. But you start getting overwhelmed you *say* so. Okay?" Artie patted his chest pockets like he was looking for a cigarette.

"You don't smoke, detective." Although Greg thought he might start.

"I did. You didn't know me then. Leah made me quit." Artie's voice broke a little before Artie straightened up and moved toward the door. "Come on. Time's a-wastin' I guess."

Greg suddenly wanted a kiss, something telling him that things would never be the same again, that once he left this room, things would be... stained. He didn't ask, though, because sometimes he was wrong.

He grabbed his coat, scratched Duke's ears. "I'm ready."

"I'm not." Artie turned back again, that lightning fast pivot stunning him again, just like it had the first time. Artie grabbed him, just like the man had heard his thoughts, and kissed him silly, lips bruising his.

He just held on tight, took it all and demanded more. So long. He'd wanted Artie for so long.

Artie just kept on and on, only stopping once little spots swam in front of his eyes, pulling back so they could whoop for breath. "Not letting you go," Artie said.

"Good." He met Artie's eyes, serious as he'd ever been. "Don't."

Nodding, Artie took his hand and they headed out the door, the two of them going together this time. Not one of them following.

He got into the car, closed his eyes. He knew that Jerry - the man's name was Jerry - wouldn't be watching this time. This time Jerry had Leah.

Artie gunned it, driving a little too recklessly, a little too fast. The man always did that when he was upset.

The building wasn't anything special. Just another gray building in another street with big houses made into little sleazy apartments. Nothing overwhelming or evil. They went to the third floor, Artie unsealing the tape and letting him in, carefully clearing the room first.

He reached for the doorknob, eyes wide as he was flooded with a sudden sense of pain, of fury, of a dull fear. "Leah. Leah hurt him. Leah hurt him, Artie."

"Good." Artie's face looked like stone, the man standing in the middle of the room with those arms crossed. "Good."

He slipped his shoes off, stepped onto the floor, fighting his gag reflex as wave after wave of shit hit him.

"Collector. He's a collector. There's a box of them, and he's trying to make a perfect one, and he has been trying for years, years. Fuck me. They're under concrete. Away. A drive. Fuck."

"A perfect what? Woman?"

"Yes. Perfect. Oh, God. Parts. He takes parts. He thinks I can..." The son of a bitch thought he could put them together. Keep them alive. He reached for the piles of books, knees buckling as he heard the women screaming. Artie grabbed his hands, strength pouring into him, all of Artie's determination to stop this guy bucking him up. "Red lights. Red lights and he found it at a... A job. His job. Underneath." Where was the fucking desk? He needed to see the desk. "The desk. The maps. The desk."

"Here. Over here." They stumbled to the desk, Artie pulling him up and staggering with him.

His hands landed flat on the wood, his spine feeling like it was going to snap in two. He scrabbled wildly, looking for the papers, for the plans. The plans in the... "Here. Here. Plans. Here. They're here."

"Okay. Okay." Artie yanked him away. "I've got them. Got them."

Artie's phone rang, the whistle and happy little tune enough to drive him mad.

"Yeah?" Poor Artie sounded rough, voice echoing from far away.

It was him. Jerry. Greg reached up, took the phone. "What do you want?"

"You, Greg. You have a gift I need." The voice was sibilant, low, smooth. Controlled.

"Is the detective okay?"

"Leah. Oh, God, Leah..." Artie flopped down next to him on the floor, hand sliding around his waist.

"She's in pain, Greg. She'll be in worse pain if you don't give me what I want."

He shook his head. "Don't hurt her. I want you to let Detective McAdams talk to her, then we'll make a deal."

"Oh, God." Poor Artie. The man was having a worse time of it than he was. Artie took the phone. "Leah? Leah, honey?" He could just hear the hint of her voice, feel the dull fury that was building up in Artie. "You hang in there," Artie was saying. "You hang in. We'll get you. No! Damn it, you bastard..."

Fuck. Fuck. "Ask him where he wants to make the trade."

"When and where?" Artie barked. "Uh-huh. Yeah. Yeah, okay. She'd better be whole."

Greg nodded, struggled to his feet so he could look around. Okay. Okay, he needed to remember it all.

The phone clunked down on the desk, Artie coming up to him, hand on him to steady him. "He hung up. Tell me, babe. Just tell me what you see."

"Red lights. Water. He worked there. He found it at a job, and they're buried close by. Big equipment. Leah shot him in the shoulder. He watches them for days before he picks them out. He watched us. Me. There's film, in my house, here, there. Cameras. Electricity."

"Oh, Jesus." Artie growled it. Growly Artie. Out in full force. "But if he worked there we can track it down."

"Where will we meet him? Will he bring Leah?" He didn't want to be here anymore.

"He says he will. He gave me some instructions. Can you stand here while I write them down?"

"Yeah. Yeah, I can." He felt filthy, like he'd never get clean again.

"Okay. I'll get the plans, just be a minute." Artie disappeared and the sickening, lurching sensation intensified crazily.

Greg wandered, bouncing from here to there, everything in him firing with too much information, too much pain, too much shit.

Then Artie was back, guiding him toward the door almost faster than his shaky legs could carry him. "Come on. Come on, man."

"I. I can't. I don't." He was just babbling, the same words over and over again.

"Greg." That voice cut right through his racing mind, Artie's hold firm, commanding. "Come on. Out. We're going home."

Greg looked over at Artie, trying to think, to figure out what they were doing, where they were. "Home."

"Yes. Home." They went down a set of stairs, out to the street where the traffic sounded loud, raucous.

He brushed against the railing at the bottom, then jerked away, landing against the side of the building as he screamed, everything just too loud, too sharp, too much.

"Shit. Come on, babe. Please." Hands yanking at his, Artie pulled him, put him in the Camaro, where it was like being surrounded by a bubble.

Everything melted into a pure, total silence.

When he could hear again, Artie was slapping his cheeks lightly, pulling at his shirtfront. "Greg. Come on, babe. We're home. Please. Come on."

"Don't be scared, Artie. You'll find her." He didn't feel like he was in his body anymore. "You give me to him and get her to a doctor."

"No." Artie shook him. Hard. "I come back with both of you. Come on. Upstairs."

He stumbled out of the car, realizing suddenly that he'd left his shoes back there.

And it was cold.

And wet.

When had it gotten wet?

Sleepwalking, he went up with Artie, who let him in and pushed him through the door, Duke coming over like a shot to wrap around his ankles.

Greg sort of crumpled, landing half in Artie's chair, half on the floor.

"I got you. We got you." He heard Artie moving, heard things clinking and closing, then Artie was back with a glass of juice. "Here. Drink up."

"'M sorry." He loved the smell of oranges. He really did.

"Not your fault, babe. No matter what that fucker tries to make you think. Not at all." Artie's hands helped him lift the cup, helped him find his mouth.

He sputtered over the first gulp, but then the right, good, bright taste of it hit him, and he drank it down.

"Good. Good. Like that. All right. Better?" The cup went away when it dried up and Artie stroked his hair, his cheek.

"Better. When... when do I have to go?" He pushed into the touch, let himself feel something good.

"Not today. Tomorrow." There was something...he frowned. He couldn't figure out what it was in Artie's voice, but there was something.

He reached out, fingers settling on Artie's wrists, those thick fingers.

Artie was hoping he was too out of it to read him. Too far gone to know that Artie had no intention of offering him up for a trade. None.

"Artie. You have to. You have to help her." It occurred to him, suddenly, that making the argument that he was going to be fine was less than logical, given he was still halfway on the floor.

"I will. I'll get her back." Restless, edgy, Artie hauled him up and put him on the chair, patting him clumsily. "But not with you."

"Then we need to find her. Find the place. He'll have her there." God, he couldn't think.

"We have the plans. We know it was a work location. I need to go call that in, babe." Artie let go, walking away, and it left him feeling cold.

He stared at Duke, who stared right back. There had to be something. Something he missed.

All sorts of thoughts nibbled at the edges of his brain, but none of them would take shape. Duke finally leapt up on his lap, purring, sharp claws kneading his thigh.

"Hey." He let his hands sink into Duke's fur, stroking and petting.

Not thinking. He was getting good at not thinking.

***

They had the whole thing set up. They were meeting with Daniels. Artie was pretty sure the fucker wasn't straying too far from his bolt hole, and they had turned up three possible work sites within two miles of the meet. They were gonna have unmarked cars and plainclothes guys on every one of them.

Two days. Two fucking days had passed since the bastard had snatched Leah. She'd better be all right. If she wasn't, Artie was going to tear the little prick to shreds. And piss on the pieces.

He straightened his tie, looking at his own haggard face in the mirror. Now all he had to do was go lie to Greg.

Jesus.

Artie went out to the living room, staring from the hallway a minute, watching Greg stare off into space and pet Duke. The damned fool was so determined to go, so fucking ready to give himself up. The captain had agreed with Artie, though. Greg shouldn't be anywhere near the supposed exchange.

"Hey. I have to go scout some. You gonna be okay until I come back and pick you up for the main event?"

"Do you think you found the right spot?" Greg had stopped having anything resembling emotion, just sinking deeper and deeper into this huge blankness. "Should I come help?"

"No!" Artie breathed deep, cursing the psycho who thought this was a great game over and over. "No. I'm good. I'll come back for you when it's time."

"Okay." Greg stood, headed toward him, eyes focused somewhere past his head.

Artie backed away. He didn't...couldn't let Greg touch him, Couldn't let the man know what he was about to do.

Greg stopped, blinked, looked at him. "Artie?"

"I. Babe. I gotta go." He couldn't help it. That look fucking crushed him. Artie held out a hand kinda helplessly.

Greg's eyes searched his face - so dark, so serious - then he got a single nod. "You be careful out there, detective, okay?"

"Okay. Yeah. I got that. Careful." Fuck, he was babbling. Shoving his hands in his pockets, Artie fumbled for the keys to the Camaro. "I'll be back soon, yeah?"

"Yeah." Greg watched him jitter and fumble, just quiet and still as stone.

Not even looking, Artie turned and left. If he looked at Greg again...well, it would all be over. Boom. So he left, Duke's accusing rumble ringing in his ears.

As soon as he got to the car he gunned the engine and got on the horn. "This is Detective McAdams. Let's do it."

He was so focused on the road and his destination that he didn't even see the tall figure that slipped out the door and into the taxi that pulled up to the curb.

They had it all figured out. As soon as the guy even showed hide or hair of Leah, they were taking him down. Getting her out of there. Hell, they had SWAT and snipers and shit.

He pulled into the parking lot of the drive-in, the damned thing old and overgrown, and shit, this would've been easier if they'd mowed.

He sat for a minute, hands on the steering wheel, trying to brace himself for what was coming. One hand went to the knot of his tie, the heel of his palm pressing against the vest he wore under his shirt.

Time always went so fucking slow at moments like this. His cell phone rang, Leah's number coming up.

He snapped it open, growling his hello. "Where is Greg?" the voice on the other end asked. "You don't get the bitch until I get Greg."

He looked over to one of the unmarked cars, a man in the backseat looking enough like Greg to pass, even at a decent distance.

"And you don't get to see him until you make nice. You know he's alive and well. I don't know that about my partner. He's here. Now show me Leah."

"At the concession stand. You see her? She's on the roof."

Artie squinted, trying to make out the figure up there, assess any booby traps.

It took a minute, then the faded light caught on Leah's hair, the duct tape over her mouth. Bingo.

He considered carefully, making sure there was no way she could be strapped to a bomb or anything. That didn't seem the guy's style, but you had to be careful. Artie got out of the car, getting his radio out. "Okay, bring out Greg," he said, hoping to God their ruse worked.

"I want him to walk toward the screen."

"Sure, but I come with him. I don't have my gun on me."

"No. You go get the bitch before I blow her head off. Greg comes to me."

The decoy was a cop, was trained for this. Artie just nodded, keeping the phone and radio open. "Okay. Okay, I'm going to get her."

"Smart man. Tell me, detective, did you kiss him goodbye?"

His teeth ground. He didn't have to fake his fury. It was right there on the surface. "You sick fuck. We'll get you, you know. One way or the other."

So close. He could see Leah's face now. She was watching him, looking just about as pissed as he'd ever seen her. He headed for one side of the building, but her head shook, warning him away.

"You'll start, but I'll have him first, detective. Come here, Dr. Pearsall. Come play with me."

That sing-songy thing ran up his back like sandpaper, making him shudder, and Artie put on some speed, trying to get to Leah before Jerry realized what was going on, before he knew he'd been duped. All he had to do was get up there now, on the roof.

Leah was struggling now, taped to a chair, bruised as all get out, fighting to get to him, get free.

That's it. Good girl. Artie hauled himself up, feet dangling, knowing this was the crucial moment when he was too vulnerable to fight back. Fucking A, it passed, though, and he was up there, pulling Leah over, chair and all, getting them down below the lip of the roof before all hell broke loose.

"You mother *fucker*!" A volley of gunshots rang out, Leah throwing herself to one side. "Where IS HE?"

Artie scrabbled, covering Leah as best he could, praying to God his vest could stop any flak that came their way.

He got the tape off Leah's hands and she tugged the tape off her mouth. "He's got an old blue Caddy, my pistol, and a semi-automatic. He's down on the far side."

"Got it." Artie found his handheld three feet away, barking orders to the uniforms and SWATs, ducking again as chips of concrete fell in his hair.

"I don't know if I can walk, Art. Bastard broke my ankle."

"We'll work it, honey." He looked at her, really looked, cataloging bumps and bruises.
"How's...how's the. You're still..."

"Still. Hell, I felt the little fucker *kick* at him when he touched me." Her eyes met his. "I want to go home, Art. I need to see Tim."

"Of course. I know they'll be clamoring to debrief you, babe, but we'll get you home." He needed to get home to Greg, too. Tell him. Well, tell him what? The shooting had stopped, but that wasn't necessarily good. Artie called it in. "Report."

"Frank took four to the jacket. Perp scrambled, you have a visual?"

"No. Goddamn it, where is he?" Artie worked the tape off Leah's ankles, trying not to take skin with it. Man, that looked raw.

"Don't let him go; he'll be pissed as hell." Leah sobbed as he touched her ankle. Damn. Damn. They were going to need an ambulance over here.

"I've got an injury. We'll need an EMT. Give me the subject's location, damn it."

"Anyone have him? Christ! Anybody?"

There were thirty-five voices jabbering all of a sudden, cops and SWAT and shit all jabbering.

"Jesus fucking Christ." Artie peered carefully over the lip of the roof, searching the ground.

"Gotta love a clusterfuck, huh?" Leah chuckled, moving beside him. "Did you bring me a weapon?"

"Here, take my spare." Unstrapping his ankle harness, Artie handed over his spare weapon, still searching, clearing the danger zones before trying to move Leah down.

"You're my best friend." Leah took it, eyes sharp. "Shit. The Caddy's gone. How the fuck is the Caddy gone?"

"We need to get moving, honey. Come on." He planted his shoulder under her arm, half carrying her to the edge of the roof that had the little metal awning. "I need to get Greg."

"You brought him here?"

"No. I left him at home. But I need him to be safe. Help me out here, guys." He could lower her, but not all the way.

"Careful now. Christ, I'm like a big pregnant target, assholes, hurry up!" Well, she hadn't lost her sense of humor.

They got her down and Artie shimmied to the ground, too. He was pretty sure their bird had flown the coop.

The head of the SWAT team came over. "We got shots fired from that overgrown area, but that's it. We never made visual contact."

"Get Leah to the hospital, and get her husband in there with her. I'm going to secure his original target."

"Artie! Artie!" Leah looked over, red spots on her cheeks. "He took me to a deserted building, not finished. He has this thing underground."

"Can you get someone there, babe? Can you describe it?" He knew they needed to go, clean that bastard's collection out.

"I'll try. I couldn't see much, but I'll try." Fuck, she was a strong broad.

"Okay. Good." He patted her shoulder clumsily. "I'll see you as soon as I get Greg, okay?"

"Okay, Art. Get the doc."

He nodded once and he was off, his car just where he left it, no bullet holes to be seen. He took off like a bat out of hell, really pushing it to get home.

There wasn't a Cadillac, no pickup. That made him feel better. Sort of. He took the stairs two at a time, wheezing as he got to his floor, the strain really getting to him now. The door seemed to take a fucking age to unlock, but Artie got it, throwing open the door.

"Greg!"

Duke yowled, the sound wicked and haunting, claws scratching viciously on his couch.

"Duke! Jesus. Quit it." Artie looked in the kitchen, the bathroom, and then the bedroom, his heart racing. No Greg. Where the fuck was Greg?

Shit. Shit. The man's jacket was gone, shoes. Fuck. He looked around, then grabbed the phone and hit redial.

It rang and rang, then a women's voice sounded, "Yellow Cab. Can I help you?"

He knew they wouldn't give him the address Greg had gone to. Not without a warrant. Artie mumbled, "Wrong number," and hung up. Where the hell would Greg go? He hadn't been at the scene. Artie knew that much. He would have known. Somehow.

Goddamn it. What would Greg think? What would he want?

He'd want to help. He'd want to get more information. He'd want to...Oh, fuck. Fuck a duck. Artie flew back down the stairs, nearly slamming Duke in the door in his haste. Greg had gone to the bastard's apartment.

He'd bet his life on it.

Chapter Fifteen

Fuckers.

He'll kill them all. The pregnant cunt. The blond fucker. All of them.

Trying to trick him. Trying to fool him. Trying to make him believe that imposter was Greg.

It isn't going to be this way.

It isn't.

He squeals up to his apartment complex, and runs up the door, heart pounding. The tape on the door's broken. Who...

Oh.

Oh, he knows that voice. He does.

He weighs the pistol in his hand, slips the safety off. He doesn't want to kill Greg. He doesn't. But he will. He's ready to.

There are two options. Cooperate or die.

***

He'd taken peyote when he was an undergrad, and the dull swirling of color and heat and sound had been like this.

The red light blinked, over and over, the soft sound of splashing and laughing and murmuring a strange constant companion. Greg groaned, shifted, frowning as he tried to move, tried to remember where he was.

What he'd touched.

God.

He shifted his hands, eyes flying open as a scream rocketed through his head. Pain. Pain. Oh, God. Oh. No.

It was too much, too much to contain and he convulsed, hands tugging at the bonds, eyes rolling in his head.

He felt the sting in his arm distantly, the heat there sliding through him, relaxing his muscles.

"That's right, Dr. Pearsall, don't struggle, you'll hurt yourself. Just relax while I pack." Pack? Pack what? He didn't understand. "Your filthy little detective fucked everything up for us. Everything."

Artie wasn't filthy. He hated ties, but he was very clean. He vacuumed twice a week to get rid of Duke's hair.

"I had wanted you to teach me. They said no one understood anatomy like you did. No one. But you wouldn't speak to me. So, I spoke with a friend who shared similar interests, and we went to speak with you, and look what you made us do." Greg frowned, trying to follow along, trying to remember how to think.

To breathe.

Oh.

Man.

Breathing was good.

Dimly he came to realize the red light was the same one from his visions, exactly the same, along with the dripping and the...oh, God. Yes, now he knew.

Leah. Oh, God. Make this mean Artie got Leah.
"Not... not helping you."

The little bastard picked up a scalpel, plopped it
in a bag. "Yes, you will. You were made for this.
You were made for me."

Made for him. No, that would be the...the thing.
The one he was collecting for. The thought made
him gag. And that made the asshole laugh.

He shook his head, swallowed hard. Okay.
Okay. What would Artie do?

Oh, man. Artie.

Artie'd never fucking find him here.

Just about the time he thought that, the little shit
happily packing away stopped moving, head
tilting.

Now, if he'd gone from picking up things to
transmitting them, Greg was fucked.

"Stop moaning, Doctor. Did you hear that?" A
gun. That was a gun, not a scalpel. Leah's gun.

"Hear what?" He didn't hear a goddamn thing.
He didn't think. Fuck. He took a deep breath, threw
his head back and hollered. "He's got a *gu-u-u-u-u-
u-u-un*!"

There. Nobody was going to hear anything now.

The gun in question smacked across the side of
his face. He thought something in his cheek
cracked. The echo was still ringing when someone
cursed viciously and things crashed down off the
little table set up with surgical tools.

Little traces of things started seeping in past the
main song of "ow" and "fuck" and "gag." Greg
thought that the kindest thing anyone could do was
shoot out that fucking blinky light.

The pop-pop of gunfire finally focused him, everything else flying out of his head as he strained to hear above the ringing in his ears.

The light started swinging, then screams started, low and furious, Jerry's hand landing on his leg, his bare hand. "No. No. Don't touch me. Don't touch me. Get off. Get off!"

He kicked out, horror and hysteria and a vague blackness soaking into him, feet connecting against Jerry with a thud.

The hand went away, Jerry's shouting all he could hear, and then a great, bearlike roar. He jerked, tugged, eyes dropping closed, the whole thing simply too much to bear, to understand.

When all of the echoes ended there was a hand on him again, just lightly touching his leg. It was not Jerry's hand. He pulled away, whimpering a little, confused. Come on, Greg. Open your eyes. You're not dead yet. Open your eyes.

"Greg. Babe." It seemed so far away, that voice.

"Artie. He has a gun. He has a gun. Artie." His eyes rolled, and he started shaking.

"Not anymore, babe. It's okay. It's okay now." Artie touched him again, this time holding him still. "You're gonna hurt yourself."

"I can't. I have to." Shit. Stop. Breathe. Whatever he'd been given kept him from fighting, kept him from having any strength. Muscle relaxant. He knew about those. They gave them to him in hospitals when he couldn't cope.

"Greg." Rough palms landed on either side of his face, Artie holding him, looking into his eyes. "You have to stop fighting so I can untie you. Tell me you understand."

"Artie." Oh, God. It was him. Really. "Leah? You found Leah?"

"She's safe. Her and the rugrat both." Artie had a trickle of blood running down his face, his expression one big grimace. He was wearing a tie. It was up under his right ear.

"Good. You hate ties." Greg loved the man so much it hurt. "I need out of this chair."

"I do. I'm getting there. Hold still, babe." Artie called him babe a lot. It was cute. He'd seen Artie call Duke babe once by mistake. It had ended in blood. Blood. Artie had blood on him.

"Artie?" He moved away from the touch, frowned, trying to understand. "You're hurt? He hurt you?"

"It's not all mine, babe. I… You'd better be careful what you touch. There's his blood kinda everywhere." Artie grimaced suddenly, turning away, his shoulders heaving.

He slid right out of the chair without the support of the detective or his own muscles and onto the floor with a splash.

He discovered he might have a limit to how much he could take in.

"Greg? Greg..." Artie seemed even farther away, but couldn't be because Artie was lifting Greg like a rag doll, hauling him down some sort of tunnel.

His head rolled and he thought he'd just keep Artie, now. Especially when they left that fucking blinky light behind.

"Just a little more, love. God knows, the uniforms should be here soon. And our guy isn't going anywhere." Somewhere in that statement was something he should be upset about.

"Uniforms. You broke your arm when you were eight on a bicycle and you didn't cry and your father brought you ice cream."

"I did. And now I have a hole in that same arm, babe. Can you walk just a little more?" Was he walking now? He wasn't sure.

"He gave me a shot." He kept trying to think about walking, trying to get the feet-legs-hips thing working.

"What was it, Greg? I know you can tell if you think hard." Oh, Artie had such faith in him. That rang *loud*.

"Muscle relaxant. He... he knew. He knew about the hospital. They gave me Flexeril and Demerol." Made him feel melted and loosey-goosey.

"Okay." He could see light now. Real light. Not the red blinky. "Do you need to go to the doctor, Greg? I need to know."

"I... I can't. I can't. I can't." He knew he should. He knew, but he simply couldn't.

"Okay. It's okay. We can have an EMT look at us both, all right? Someone will have to make the report." Now there was a flashing red light again, but it was outside.

"What is with the fucking red lights!" He really, really was tired of this whole day.

"Those are ambulance lights, babe." Oh, he knew that voice. The tone. The humor. The lunatic thing.

"Don't. Don't treat me like I'm crazy." He wasn't crazy. He wasn't. He was tired. Sick. Homeless. "I'm not crazy!"

"I know that!" Artie snarled it, grabbing his upper arms and shaking him. "You almost died!"

Greg simply lost it, the edges of reality and not blurring and fading away as he flailed and shattered into a million pieces.

Enough.

He had had enough.

Chapter Sixteen

Artie was fucking exhausted. He'd fought taking Greg to the hospital, leaving Greg with Alice and Mitch at his place while he went in for the standard gunshot exam, and then on to being drilled on the discharging of his own firearm. Over and over and over again.

He'd been patched up, cleaned off, and given leave with pay for a week. At least.

When he came back, though, Leah would be on short hours. They'd decided that was best. He hated it, but there it was.

His door looked almost ominous when he stopped outside it. His arm throbbed, and his ribs hurt, and he was afraid to try to close his eyes and sleep... afraid of what he'd see.

Artie took a deep breath and put his key in the lock, heading in.

The sound Duke made was three parts fury and one part rage, the yowl warning him before sixteen pounds of furious Siamese tackled him at the door.

Mitch looked over from the dining room table where he was dealing cards. "Detective. You're home."

Ah, Mitch. Mr. Obvious.

"Shit! Duke, come on, man. I'm injured." His hands got scratched to hell as he reached down to pry Duke off him, dangling the suddenly dead kitty weight. "Don't everyone help me at once."

"Artie, dear. I adore you, but that cat is demon possessed." Alice came out of the kitchen, drying her hands on a towel. "He's bitten Mitch twice and howled at Dr. Nyguen when he came to see Greg. Would you like some tea?"

"Yeah. They won't let me have a beer. They shot me full of stuff." Where was Greg? He had to be there. Artie wandered in, still holding Duke, fingers petting automatically.

"Well, I hope you didn't drive. Mitch, help Artie get settled on the sofa, love?" Alice just pottered, heading back into to the kitchen.

"I..." he stuttered, looking at Mitch like a deer in the headlights. "I need to see Greg."

Mitch shook his head. "Greg's sleeping, Artie. Dr. Nyguen gave him stuff and told us to leave him alone."

"I won't touch him. I won't even get close enough to disturb his fucking brainwaves. I just need to see him." Plopping Duke on the couch, he headed for the bedroom, reeling a little.

"Uh. Alice? Love?" Mitch sort of... fluttered behind him.

"Let it be, Mitch. Artie won't hurt him. Come reach teacups for me."

Did he have teacups?

Greg was wrapped up on his bed like a mummy, a white sheet cocooning and swaddling Greg like a papoose or something. All Artie could see was Greg's face, bruised and swollen on one side.

He swallowed hard, moving just far enough into the room to see Greg's chest rising and falling, moving all that bedding. Oh. Oh, thank God.

"Artie." Greg's eyes were still closed, but that was his name, slurred and lost.

"Right here, babe. Right here. It's all fine. Sleep." God, he loved that man. So much.

"Love you. Come to bed, Artie. Duke is hungry."

"Do you think Alice will give him tea and cakes?" Artie shrugged carefully out of his coat, his arm stabbing at him, feeling like Duke was clawing out from the inside. Shoes, shirt, pants...his stupid tie was in the trash. Artie crawled on the bed.

"I hope not. I fucking hate that tea."

"I don't think I have teacups. Do you think they might have been here when I moved in?" Oh. Greg. Against him. Artie nuzzled the poor bruised cheek so lightly even Duke would be proud.

"Maybe. The doctor promised I wouldn't dream."

"You're not dreaming, babe." Okay, he was babbling, he could see why it would seem dreamlike. "I'm right here. Can you feel me?"

"Yeah. Inside me. Like a good drug. Is Leah's baby okay?"

"So far so good. They want her to take it easy." They wanted him to, also. He knew now what Greg felt like with the crazy talking.

"Are you in trouble? At work? Because of me?" Greg managed to roll over, pressing against him.

"No. They're just very careful around the guy with the loose cannon." He sighed, his eyes sliding closed.

"Oh." Greg sighed, too, breath moving the hair at his temple. "No dreams, Artie."

"No. We'll guard each other's backs." No dreams. Please, God. Just let them rest.

Just for one night.

***

Greg opened his eyes when Alice entered the room and Artie sat up, flailing, reaching for the bedside table.

"Easy. Easy. I just wanted to tell you we're going home. Greg needs his medicine." Alice looked tired, worn. "I'm going to open the store."

"I need to pee. Help me out of this." God, his voice sounded like he'd gargled sandpaper.

Artie blinked, staring down at him, then at Alice. "Where...what?"

"It's okay. Should I leave Mitch? He can help. Make tea."

"God no. Just unwrap me."

Artie finally looked at him, comprehension dawning. "Oh. Hey, babe. Hey, Alice." Like an archaeologist unwrapping a mummy, Artie started getting him loose.

"Hey." He tried to help, wiggling some, trying to not freak out about being trapped.

"It's okay, babe," Artie said, tongue sticking out as he worked. If he focused on that, it was kind of cute and distracting.

"How's your arm?" He could feel the urge to float away, to just close his eyes and drift.

"Kinda sore." Artie peered into his face. "You okay? Do you need something?"

"Just a little floaty. What did they give me?"

Alice sighed. "Baclofen and Flexeril with a shot of Demerol and Phenergan. You went down hard."

"I suppose I did."

"Well, we got you now." Artie gave him a little smile, bruises coming to light along one cheek. "There. All set. See, you're free."

"Yeah." He tried to smile back and stopped as his cheek screamed out. Oh. Oh, okay. So none of that shit. Damn. "I have to pee." He stood up, wavering a little as Alice came close. "Don't! Don't fucking touch me. I can't."

"It's okay, Alice," Artie said, sitting up with a groan and reaching out to pat Alice's hand. "If he's on his feet, you and Mitch are safe to go. Thank you so much."

"Okay. Okay, Greg. I'm sorry, honey." Oh, for Christ's sake. Don't cry.

"Yeah. I'm just edgy. Go make us money, beautiful." His teeth were floating; if he didn't get to the bathroom soon, he was going to do his impersonation of a water sprinkler.

Artie stood, wrapping a sheet around his waist. "Come on, hon. I'll walk you out. Greg can motivate to the head on his own. Holler if you need me, babe."

"Yeah." He made it to the bathroom, careful not to touch any of Artie's clothes, any of the towels the doctor had used, anything but the faucet, the toilet paper, the handle. His breath eased as nothing set him off.

By the time he got back out Alice was gone. Artie was nowhere to be seen in the bedroom, either, only Duke, delicately picking his way through the covers and sniffing.

"Hey, man. Did you get your pound of flesh off Mitch?" He settled on the edge of the mattress, hand held out for Duke.

Duke came right to him, bright Siamese eye focused on him, cheek stroking against his fingers.

"Mmm." He smiled, relaxed, scratching those soft ears, humming low.

"Hey." Artie stood in the doorway, regarding him and Duke with a fond, if wary, expression. "Better?"

"Yeah. I'm sorry. I just... I couldn't let her." He scratched his way along Duke's spine, focusing on that happy spot at the base of his tail.

"I know. She's all right. Just worried."

Duke did that kitty ecstasy thing, arching, good eye fluttering. Artie laughed, the sound oddly loud in the quiet room. Duke purred like a motor.

"That's right. It feels good, yeah, Duke?" He looked up at Artie, knowing that he looked sort of monstrous, with the bruising and swelling.

"Feels good to know that something can still feel... uh... good."

"Yeah." The edges of Artie's mouth curled up in a funny grin. "I'd show you, but we're both beat to hell. How about food? I bet that will help with the pleasure principle. I know it will for me."

"No meat." He nodded, even though he wasn't sure he was hungry. "I could make eggs."

"Sure. I can help. Butter toast." Finally, Artie moved, coming close, not touching, but close. They shared a touch of sorts through Duke, who graciously allowed Artie to scratch his chin.

"And salmon for Duke. Alice probably fed him something horrible and organic."

"That must be why he tried to take off my shin." Oh, ow. That cat was going to be the death of Artie for sure. It must be love.

"Probably." He stood up, looking for Artie's shorts. The soft ones.

Pointing him toward the chest of drawers, Artie dropped the sheets and headed into the bathroom, coming back a minute later, scratching his belly. "Damn. I'm all fuzzy."

"You look good." He felt... shattered. Literally. Like he was made of glass and had been slammed against the floor.

"I look like a three-day binge. Come on, babe. Food." Artie wandered out into the hallway, still naked as a jaybird.

"Shake it, detective." He followed, frowning at all the things Alice had cleaned, moved.

"She didn't touch my chair," Artie said, as if he'd heard. Even Artie's ass had a bruise on it. But he got a nice show as Artie jiggled, just for him.

"Good. I love that chair." Greg made his way to the kitchen, the whole thing spotless. Shining. Alice-ized. "Throw that tea away, would you?"

"Uh-huh. Nasty." Pots and pans rattled as Artie set him up for egg making, then moved to dump the pot of tea in the sink. "Knowing my luck, Duke will crave it now."

"You think? We'll tempt him away with tuna." He found the salt and pepper, a fork. It was almost normal.

Sort of.

"Yeah. The good stuff. You don't think he'll get mercury poisoning or anything do you?" Only Artie would worry about that.

"I don't think so. He might be able to eat thermometers like pretzel sticks and be okay."

"This is true. He's not really a cat. He's a demon in kitty clothes. I bet he has stomach acid like brimstone." They grinned at each other, the familiar banter easing their way.

"Yes. Thank goodness he's on our side." He looked down at Artie's ankles, all scratched and torn up. "Usually."

"He was kinda pissy at me." The bread was a little moldy. Artie rummaged in the freezer and handed him some bagels for bread instead.

"Do you know... I mean, what *day* is it? How long did everything take to happen?"

"I knew before I went to bed. I had to date those forms. I'm on leave..." He got a kind of helpless look. "I don't know, babe."

"Me either." Greg looked back. "We'll watch the news... when it comes on. Next."

"Yeah. I don't know...it's three." The little clock on the microwave said three.

"Well, Alice was dressed and the sun is up, so it has to be afternoon."

"Oh, good. Right." The food actually started to smell good, the simple smells of yeast and eggs and stuff really making him hungry.

They got the food plated up, got settled, him in Artie's chair, Artie on the old plaid sofa, both of them quiet and eating, forks clicking and sliding on the china.

Artie kept sneaking peeks at him, gray eyes rising and then falling. A couple times it looked like Artie might say something, but just didn't.

He knew how Artie felt. He wanted... Hell, he didn't fucking know what he wanted.

He wasn't sure he'd be able to do if he did.

Finally Artie sighed and put his plate aside, patting his belly. "Good, babe."

"Yeah." He nodded, curling up in the chair, cheek on one arm, legs sprawling. "I was starving."

Artie got up and came over, settling on the floor next to the chair, head leaning back next to his face. Close, but not touching.

"Hey." He could smell Artie and it was right. It was just... Yeah.

"Hey. Fuck, babe, it's been a long couple of days." The man had a talent for understatement.

"Yeah. Yeah, you could say that." He nodded, the action brushing his lips against the top of Artie's head.

The man all but purred for him, that tiny touch drawing a shiver. "I could," Artie agreed, "but Duke would claw me for repeating myself."

"I wouldn't want that." He watched his hand as it slid over his own chest, heading for Artie.

Leaning into his touch before it even came, Artie smiled for him, eyes sliding closed. "We could go back to bed. Nothing energetic. Just a nap."

"Yeah. Yeah, we could. I... Yeah, Artie. We need to rest."

"We do. The rest can wait, you know?" For now. It was unspoken, but left in the air.

"Yes. It's going to have to."

"Okay." Rolling to his feet, Artie stood and held a hand down to him. "We'll leave the dishes."

He reached up, hand slapping into Artie's, the random thoughts and images panicking him for a second before they eased into something closer to normal.

"Love you," Artie said, looking him right in the eye. Greg could feel everything between them coalesce into those two words, Artie meaning them with everything in him.

Yeah. The rest could wait.

Chapter Seventeen

Artie wandered.

He wasn't sure what else to do. He was still on leave, and when he'd called in to ask about coming back, the cap had reamed him but good. He figured that was a big old no.

All he'd done to get him out of the house was grocery shop, replacing the macrobiotic shit Alice had gotten them with pork rinds for him and oranges for Greg and a tiny bag of lump crab meat for Duke. As, like, a make-up gift.

Now he wandered back into the living room, idly scratching his bare belly above his loose pants. At least on leave he didn't have to wear a tie.

He grabbed the phone as he passed, dialing Leah's home number, just kinda needing to hear her voice.

"Man, they haven't let you go back either? Shit, you shoot a serial psycho or get knocked up and they act like you're the bad guy." He grinned at the words - no hello, how are you, how's things, just right back into it. "How's the doc?"

"He's okay..." Looking fragile and disconnected, but better, maybe. Hell, who knew. "How's the panicky hubby?"

"Panicky. He fusses every time I get up to go to the friggin' bathroom. He felt the baby kick yesterday, though. They're pretty sure it's a girl."

"Oh, good. She'll be kick ass." He grinned a little, flopping down in his chair. Greg was in the kitchen, Artie could hear the clatter of something. "Did you finally get in to make your report?"

"Yeah. I'm on short hours until February, then gone until six weeks after the baby comes. They're punishing me for not waiting for backup. They tell you that the guy'd been watching Greg for years, man? Just waiting?"

The little hairs on the back of his neck rose, even though he had known that. It fucked him up every time. "Yeah. Sick fuck. What he did to those girls."

"Yeah. They identified the last victim. A cherry reporter from KWAX. Virginia something. Looks like he was the leak. Called it in to catch her."

"Poor kid." He'd never lost any love for reporters, but no one deserved to die in pieces. "Anything you need, honey?"

"Real fucking coffee and for Tim to get his ass back to work."

Lord, he did love that woman. "Yeah, well, I can't help you with either. But I can offer commiseration on the forced leave thing. Just think of Lavaca and Jones having to take our cases."

Her laugh rang out, made him grin. "Oh, hell, yes. I dare that stupid bastard to decipher your handwriting. Kiss the doc for me and come visit. We'll compare battle scars."

"Will do." That would be a good thing, going to see Leah. And he'd bet Greg could use some alone time. The man was way more solitary than Artie. "See you in a bit."

"I'll be here." He heard her telling Tim he was going to visit as the phone hung up. Artie bet Tim would love that shit.

Rolling to his feet, Artie padded into the kitchen to put a hand on Greg's shoulder. He made sure Greg saw him first, though. No surprises right now. "Leah wants me to come on over for a bit. She's bored."

"Yeah? I bet. Bed rest sucks." Greg had been making a fruit salad - grapes and berries and pineapple and shit. The man hadn't been able to even look at meat since. Well, since Jerry the Crazy Asshole had left presents all over Greg's place.

"Yeah, no kidding." His own arm still hurt, itched like crazy. The enforced inactivity made him insane. Artie grabbed a grape. "You gonna be good to go?"

"Yeah. I'm going to call Alice. Try to think about making some decisions for the store for the holidays."

"Cool." When Greg had told him he wasn't just going to sell the store, Artie had been kinda relieved. Greg had put a lot into that place, and it suited him. "Okay, babe. I'll take my cell. You've got the new number?"

"Yeah. Have a good time. Tell her Alice asked about her." It was like Greg wasn't even there.

The whole thing just made him fucking furious. Artie sighed. "I will, babe. C'mere and give me sugar."

That got him a smile, Greg turning to pop a raspberry into his lips before giving him a kiss, body pressed against his, nice and close.

Let that soak in a minute, he thought. Just a minute. Artie kissed back hard, holding Greg to him.

"Mmm..." It was something, the way Greg melted into him, rubbed against him.

"Yeah." That was a hell of a kiss, too, proving that Greg was in there somewhere, ready to be pulled out.

"Uh-huh." Oh. He remembered that dazed and melted look.

Pretty. Artie grinned. "Just wait until I get home. You can feed me fruit salad with your fingers."

Greg actually blushed; it was a good look. "I could really enjoy that..."

"Good. Count on it. I'll be back in about an hour and a half." Another kiss and Artie went to put on clothes before he got too wrapped up in Greg.

He heard Greg start to whistle before he was done. Oh. Oh, that was cool.

That made him smile all the way out of the apartment and halfway to Leah's. The asshole that cut him off in traffic kinda took care of it then.

Tim was out in the front yard, putting out mums and a wreath with a cornucopia. God, in a year there'd be paper turkeys and moon-faced pilgrims.

"Artie. You think you can manage not to get hurt if I let you in? Either one of you?" The words were only mostly a joke.

"I think so, man. I'm ready to go a good stretch with no shooting and/or kidnapping." He'd almost said torture, but he figured Tim might keel over.

"Go keep her company." Tim shook his head. "There's beer in the fridge. She can't have any. Or caffeine. No matter what she says."

"Yeah. Okay." Poor Leah. The door yielded easily and Artie headed in, hollering for her. "Leah? Babe?"

"In the front room, stud! You're here! I'm bored! Did you bring me ammo? There's these little kids throwing rocks at Buster and Keno in the back yard..."

"No. I did bring you decaf French Roast." So there, Tim.

"Oh, I love you." She looked good, even if the ankle was in this horrible, pinny traction deal. Man, she was sort of actually looking pregnant.

Weird.

"Do I get to rub the Buddha?" he asked, heading for the kitchen to start a pot. He'd do it just like Greg had told him to. Maybe it would come out.

"You bet. She'll kick the hell out of you. How's the arm?" Leah's kitchen made his and Greg's look sterile - so many colors and shit.

"Sore as an abscessed tooth. I could go a while without that happening again." Once the coffee maker was hissing and spitting, Artie went to sit next to Leah, putting a hand on her belly.

Oh. Oh, man. He could *feel* that baby moving. Oh, damn. Leah laughed, belly jumping under his hand. "You should see your face!"

"What? It's cool!" As he moved, the kick seemed to follow. It was fucking bizarre. But so neat.

"It is, huh? She's real." She met his eyes, winked. "You think your doc could hear her think?"

"Oh, there's a thought. I dunno." Would that freak Greg out? Was it even possible? Artie chuckled. "So you've got the guy doing yard decoration now."

"Yep. I figure I keep it up? He'll quit hovering." Wicked, evil broad.

"I know I would. Lemme get the coffee." He found some cookies in the kitchen, too. Sugar wasn't on her no-eat list as far as he knew.

She grinned at him when he came back. "Man, the doc's training you well. I like it."

"Yeah, yeah. I like cookies." He grinned back, though, relaxing a little. It felt good. Almost right.

"Mmm. Me, too. Come on. Sit. You cool? You and the doc? That dude didn't..." She swallowed, winced. "Didn't hurt him, huh?"

"No more'n you'd reckon. Not nearly as much as you, even. He just drugged Greg silly. Cracked a cheekbone."

"Good." She looked serious, like she meant it. "That dude was deeply fucked up. I can't imagine having him inside my head."

"Yeah. Yeah, maybe it was easier for Greg to be drugged. He couldn't feel as much that way. Those girls..."

"Sixteen of them, that they found." Leah met his eyes, lips tight. "We did good, Art. We stopped him."

Bile rose in his throat. That he hadn't seen in the reports. Sixteen. Jesus. "We weren't in time to save the last one, though."

"You were in time to save me. You were in time to save Greg."

"Yeah." He smiled, trying not to think of the crime scene photos. "I don't think I coulda stood losing either of you."

"We managed, and now we gotta get ready to do it again. How long are you on leave?"

"A few weeks, maybe? I don't know. I called in this morning and the cap reamed me but good." He shrugged, sipping his coffee.

"Frank's just bored. The others aren't near as entertaining as us."

"That's true enough. We get all the fun shit. The reporters have gone away, though. Did I tell you? After what happened, Alice says they've stopped hanging around the store."

"Shit, one of their own got run through by a psycho. They'll be back. They always are. You think Greg'll go back to his house?"

"I don't know. He and Alice are going to talk about the store over the holidays, and I guess we'll go from there." He loved having Greg in his place. So did Duke. But man, he needed to get out more.

"If he doesn't, y'all need a bigger place. He'll drive you bat shit crazy." She tutted, raised one hand. "Hey. Hey, no offense, man. I like the doc, but he's like... never gonna get better. He's never gonna be able to just be a guy and you can, yeah?"

"I know." He did know that. He was prepared for it. But damn, hearing it so bald like that. It made him sad. Artie had another cookie, and then another. "We'll let Duke pick a place."

"Now there's a plan. You'll end up in Wilmington, next to a fish monger with a pretty little Burmese sunning herself in the window."

Oh. A laugh burst out of his chest, and Artie just howled, laughing until he hurt. Until he had tears streaming down his face. God, yeah.

When they stopped laughing, Tim was standing in the doorway, grinning ear-to-ear. "All must be right with the world, huh, detectives?"

"You know it, baby." Leah's hand landed on her belly. "Or at least it's getting there."

"You know it, babe," Artie agreed, toasting her with his coffee cup. They'd get back to right somehow. They just didn't know how to give up. Period.

Chapter Eighteen

There was this bench in the courtyard. He could see up into the apartment through a window. He could also see into the living room through the kitchen window. And into the bathroom if he crawled onto the balcony. What he couldn't see was why he kept coming here. Why he left Artie's and walked and walked and ended up here. At Jerry Daniels' apartment.

He shivered, shook, wrapped in a denim jacket, and just watched.

The crunch of wheels on blacktop tore his intent gaze from the building, the purr of Artie's Camaro engine familiar down in his bones.

"Babe?" Artie called out the window. "Come on. What are you doing?"

"Sitting." Trying to figure this out. Trying to figure out why. "What are you doing?"

"Looking for you. I thought I'd get us a pizza. Veggie lovers."

"Oh. I'd like that." He stood up, eyes caught by those windows one more time. "It's getting cold."

"It is. You'll catch something, babe." That face he knew so well was furrowed by a frown, but Artie leaned to open the door for him, the blast of warm air from the car heavenly.

"Mmm..." He settled in, closed his eyes a second. His grandfather's scalpel was in that apartment somewhere. "Feels good."

"Yeah. It's not, you know. They took your kit to the evidence locker, and they'll release it when the full investigation is done." He hadn't said that out loud. How did Artie always know?

"You know, people are going to start wondering if you're psychic." Greg chewed on his bottom lip, rubbed his fingers together.

"Huh?" The look Artie gave him spoke volumes about how unconscious it all was. He just looked baffled.

"Nothing. How was your day?" When all else fails, sink to the banal.

"Okay." The hunched shoulders told another tale. "Hey, how about we get one of those take-and-bake things?"

"Sure." That worked. Hell, that worked just as well as anything. "That way we get the good cheese."

"Yeah. And those yummy pickled olives." They drove in silence until Artie pulled into a lot, shutting the car down and turning to him, arm along the seat. "Why, babe?"

The easiest answer was the bullshit one. Too bad he didn't think Artie would buy it. "I don't know."

"I mean, I can probably get you in there if you need to go in. I… It's just coming home with you not there and knowing you're over at his place is, I dunno. Unsettling."

"I..." There was all this shit. Tons of it. And he didn't fucking know how to handle it. "Yeah. I guess it is. I don't. I don't know."

All he could do was keep coming back to the same thoughts. How he wasn't normal. How he wasn't home. How Jerry was inside him somehow. How Artie'd gone from someone he saw three times a month to someone he saw hours every day, and maybe Artie was second-guessing that whole living with a housebound psychic thing.

Except he wasn't so much because he kept ending up at Jerry's apartment...

"Okay, babe. I'm sorry. I just. I worry about you, you know?" Artie touched him, just his shoulder.

"I do." He sighed, leaned into the touch without even thinking. He looked at the stores, the Christmas lights going up, even though it wasn't quite Thanksgiving.

"You gonna stay put if I go order?" Artie gave him a wink, a squeeze.

"Maybe. Maybe I'll go run amok and start kidnapping blondes and hacking them to little pieces." His mouth snapped shut so fast that he bit his tongue. Christ. That wasn't funny.

"Goddamn it, Greg." Those gray eyes went frosty. "Get the fuck over yourself. Okay? Jesus Christ, just don't fucking wander off." The car door slammed hard enough to rock the Camaro as Artie got out.

Get over himself. He sat for about half a minute, staring at his hands, then he wrenched the car door open, suddenly so pissed he was shaking. "Fuck this."

Who the hell did Artie think he was? Treating him like he was helpless? Stupid? He'd been surviving just fine on his own, helping, for years. Fucking *years*.

Artie came right back out like the pizza place had a revolving door, coming right for him. "Greg. Please. Come on, don't. I'm sorry."

"Stop it, Artie. Just go order your pizza. I'm going home." His home. Back where he fucking belonged if it drove him insane while he gutted it.

"And do what? Come on. Just come home with me. We'll go to your place this weekend, okay?" Artie reached for him, missed him as he drew back sharply.

"Don't. Just don't. I'm not helpless. I'm not fucking stupid. You think I wanted this? This asshole to come in and make everything filthy? To touch everything? Two months ago I hadn't left my building in a year and a half!" Was he even fucking making sense?

"No. I don't think you wanted any of this. I don't think you're stupid. I just. Fuck, Greg, I don't know what to do to make it better!"

"I don't either." He looked over at Artie, just sick and lost and fucking cold. "But I can't fucking sit in front of that apartment and worry whether or not he's left parts of him inside me."

"No. You could never be anything like him. And we'll start...we'll start getting shit together, deciding what we want to do. Stop dancing around it." Artie looked so earnest. So sincere.

"I think we will." It just wouldn't be like this, on this unequal ground, not with this... filth all around him. "I'm going home, Artie. I have to clean my house."

Artie spread his hands, shoulders hunching up again. "Does it have to be now?"

He wanted to touch Artie, to wrap himself up and hold on and found out where the fuck he was. "I don't know."

"Okay." They stared at each other until Artie finally shook his head and pointed to the car. "Get in. We'll go to your place and you can decide."

"Okay." He met Artie's eyes, just stopping for a second. "I need to know he didn't leave anything inside me. I know it's stupid, but he *touched* me, Artie."

"No. No, it's not stupid if you feel it. I trust your gut. Maybe the way to clean him out is to get your life back." That was Artie. Always trying to help, to believe.

"Maybe. Maybe. Let's... Let's get our pizza." See them. See them try to make it work.

"Sure." Artie smiled at him, the look wavering just a little. "We could get the Greek one instead of the veggie if you want. That has artichokes. Olives and shit."

"Yeah. This... this isn't about you, you know that. This isn't about not wanting you." God, he was tired of talking.

"I know. I do." Moving close, Artie nudged him with one elbow. "I know. Come on, babe."

"Yeah. Been a long fucking day somehow." Too fucking long.

"We'll get some of that cake stuff, too. With the espresso." Yeah, that would calm them down.

He reached out, grabbed Artie's hand for just a second, squeezed just to let Artie know that he was... here.

Artie squeezed back, giving him a grin that looked much more real. More old Artie. "Yeah. I get it."

And that was that.

***

The dream was one of those that Artie knew was a dream. He could sit there and watch and tell himself, "wake up, doofus," and still be scared shitless about it.

In it Greg had gone back to that bastard's apartment, and instead of being dead the guy was a walking zombie, wielding Greg's family scalpel or whatever and telling Greg he needed Greg's heart to make himself complete.

Artie finally woke up when the blade sank into Greg's chest.

He stifled his shout and lay there, his chest heaving, his hands clenched into fists to keep from reaching for Greg. He didn't need to make sure Greg was breathing, that he was whole. It was just a dream.

Greg turned his head, hands reaching out and grabbing him, tugging him into the curve of Greg's body. "A dream. A dream, Artie."

"Oh, God." He turned and clung, arms slipping around Greg's waist. This was why he tried not to dream. "Just a dream."

"Mmmhmm. He can't come back. He *can't*." Greg's legs slid between his, chin snuggled against his neck. "He can't."

"No. I know. I just..." Man, sometimes it was freaky when Greg did that. Sometimes it was comforting. Cut down on all of the whole true confessions thing.

"I know. I know, he... he wanted. Coveted. Collected. That's what he thought. He collected them."

"It still makes me twitchy, babe." The whole thought of it. God. And Greg and Leah both being in the hands of that madman.

Greg nodded, shuddered. "I hear you."

Those hands splayed over his back, rubbing a little, drawing circles. He could feel Greg trying to relax, to let it go. Artie sighed, feeling his spine stop trying to snap itself in two. He kissed Greg's throat, letting his tension slip.

"Mmm..." Greg lifted his chin, actually offering that long, pale throat to him.

So he took it, closing his eyes and feeling. It had been way too long since he'd done that. Artie let his lips trail up and down Greg's skin, let his tongue slide out to taste.

"Oh." Greg's fingers ran through his hair as the sweetest fucking moan vibrated its way out of Greg.

"Babe." Artie turned on his side a little better, making it easier to reach. They settled against each other, their bodies fitting just fine, Greg's thigh nudging his cock.

"You feel good." Greg started rocking a little, just enough to make Artie's skin heat up, his nerves wake and pay attention.

"Uh-huh. You feel amazing." Greg did. Feel amazing. Artie rubbed, all but whimpering as his favorite parts got a good bit of friction.

Greg's hands started rubbing, fingers pushing in here and there. Those amazing hands found nerves and muscles and whenever a good spot got hit, Greg *knew*.

Artie's body arched, undulated, demanding that Greg get closer right now. Immediately.

"Uh-huh. I need you, Artie." Greg's lips brushed his ear, right underneath, voice just a little desperate. "I want to feel you inside me."

"Now. Yeah. I can do that." He so could, if he could find lube. "How do you want it, babe? You want to be on top?"

"Mmm... You just like to watch me move." Oh, shit. That little sound Greg's voice made, rough and deep and pure sex, that went straight to his prick.

"I love it all, babe. Every bit." He could watch from the top, too. His arm ought to hold up. Hopefully.

"You have better things to worry about that whether your arm will hold. I want you touching me. I love your hands."

"Yeah?" At that he did lift his head to look at Greg, staring into that heated gaze. "I like to touch you."

He rolled on his back, pulling Greg with him. On top. Let Greg find the lube.

Greg laughed and started digging in the little drawer in the headboard - God, how long since he'd heard that? Just easy and happy and not tight and caught in Greg's chest?

While Greg rummaged Artie touched, sliding his hands along Greg's ribs, under Greg's arms, feeling the hot skin where it was so soft.

The sounds of digging sort of hiccuped and Greg moaned, pushing into his hands so nice. "Artie. So good."

"You are. Hot, babe." A tiny nipple rose under Artie's fingers as he pulled at it, then covered it with his palm.

He could feel Greg's heart pounding, feel the little, hard bit of flesh rubbing his hand. Greg was humming, rocking just a little, that ass making promises. The lube was pushed into his other hand, Greg just wanting. No way was he gonna fail to deliver. Artie popped the top, squirting a big blob of lube on his fingers and reaching for Greg's ass, pushing at the hot little hole there.

"Never do. You never leave me hanging. You never did, even before." Greg bore down, riding him, taking him in just so.

"Love you." It just slipped out when he wasn't thinking, but he did. He wasn't ashamed. It was just like it was. He stretched Greg carefully, fingers moving inside.

"Yes. You... Here." Greg held his hand against that thin chest, that pounding heart. "Right here. So long, Artie. Oh... Oh, there. Again."

"Here?" He pushed his fingers in, finding that same spot, pressing against it until he thought Greg was gonna buck right off the bed. Then he pulled free, yanking Greg up on top of him. "Now."

"God, yes. Now." Greg grabbed his cock, that hand firm and knowing exactly what they needed. Oh, hell, yes. Greg was tight, just burning as he was taken in deep.

He pushed up, Greg bore down, and damn. A man could be happy for life. Just like that. Artie groaned, remembering to touch, his hands slipping and sliding.

Greg nodded, lips open, hands flat on his chest. Greg looked dazed, blissed out. Damn.

Hell, Artie figured he probably looked that way, too. He slid one hand up behind Greg's head, pulling the man down for a kiss. He wanted to

taste. So bad. He got it, Greg's happy little cry
pushing into his lips a heartbeat before Greg's
tongue did.

Oh, fuck yes. Artie opened right up, let Greg's
tongue fuck his mouth the same way he was
moving inside Greg, hard and fast and burning hot.
They just moved through it, the heat flaring
between them, flaming and leaving everything else
in ashes. Like a fucking phoenix. That was what
they needed. Cleansing. Fucking A. The kiss went
crazy, their lips bruising, Greg's so soft against his
that he groaned at the feeling, humping up with his
hips.

Heat sprayed over his belly, Greg's body going
tight and milking his cock as Greg gave it up. Jesus
fuck. Artie went tight, his whole body shuddering
as he came, filling Greg deep with his spunk. God
almighty.

Greg groaned, the kiss going soft, lazy. Happy.

His fingers ran across the back of Greg's neck,
feeling the lack of tension there, the ease in the
muscles. "Mmmm. Good."

"Mmmhmm." Greg just snuggled in like they
hadn't been sleeping with careful inches between
them for days. The dam felt like it was broken, and
Artie clung like a limpet, needing the contact.
Really jonesing on it.

"When we get the place fixed, will you and
Duke come and stay? Stay there with me?"

He pondered that, not wanting to agree just to
agree. Could he live there? Yeah. If Greg was
there, and Duke, and his shit. Yeah. They'd make it
Greg's again. No. They'd make it theirs. "Yeah,
babe. Yeah. I will."

"Oh." Greg smiled, settled deep. "Oh, good. You... You're inside me."

"I am." All the way. And not just physically. "Love you, babe."

"Yeah, Artie. All of me. Think you can sleep now?"

"I think so, babe. If you stay with me." They could beat those dreams. They could. They'd figure it out together.

Epilogue

Greg heard Duke mewling before the elevator stopped, and he braced himself for the pouncing. They'd had a Christmas Eve rush - which was weird, but true. Crystals and books, jewelry and music, and that damned pyramid, all zooming out the door. It made for a happy Christmas, and as he'd squeezed Alice's hand, she'd been happy, pleased.

Now, though, it was Christmas and time to feed Duke his supper.

He got an armful of Siamese about the time that the smell of chocolate and tomato sauce hit him. "Artie? You home already?"

"In the kitchen, babe."

Oh, cool. Usually this time of year was crazy for the PD, and Artie had been getting home at all hours.

He was still getting used to the colors. The white had been replaced with warm reds in the living room and bright blues and light yellows in the kitchen. They'd done all the work themselves, had even taken half of the third floor that had been all storage and made a nice, big office for Artie, with Mitch coming in to help.

"We had a good day. Busy. Merry Christmas."

"Merry Christmas," Artie said, up to his elbows in some kind of dough. "Come on over. Don't let Duke fool you. I gave him leftover flounder."

"Oooh. What's that?" He chuckled, nuzzling the top of Duke's head. "And I don't know, he's starving."

"That's because he's spent all that energy chewing brimstone so he can breathe fire when we're not here..." Artie laughed as Duke hissed at him. "It is going to be some yummy braided parmesan bread."

They'd decided on sort of a non-traditional feast. He wasn't sure either of them would ever eat meat again.

"Ooooh." He got a dish and some cream for Duke, then went to look and smell. And wrap his arms around Artie.

"Hey." Artie grinned, bumping their heads as he tried to turn and look. "So, the business rocked, huh?"

"It did. Made us some money. How's Leah? She feeling Christmassy yet?"

"I'm not sure. She seems to be mostly taking on Duke's less desirable traits." Artie said it so cheerfully that Greg had to laugh.

"Ho ho ho?" He settled in, jonesing on the feel of Artie's muscles moving against him. "What do you need me to do?"

"The salad. The vinaigrette, too. And hey, you can uncork wine." They got maneuvered a little so Artie could kiss him without giving up kneading.

"Mmm." That was just right, and Artie agreed, a rich pleasure just right there.

When they broke apart Artie wrangled the dough onto a board and started rolling it out to braid. Artie had really gotten into the cooking for him, buying a couple of cookbooks and stuff when Artie found out how much easier it was for Greg to eat homemade food.

He started on the wine, hummed with the carols floating through the house. Between them, they had replaced, refinished, repainted everything that they didn't bring from Artie's. They were making it work.

"Man, I tell you what. Things are jumping at work. They gave me and Leah preference on days off, though. Cool, huh?"

"What is it about criminals and holidays? Do they not have enough to do?"

"I think they figure people are vulnerable then. That, and crimes of passion are high when the holidays are in. Ta da."

Oh. That bread looked...mangled. But it would taste good, he'd bet, with all that olive oil and parmesan.

He laughed and applauded, just loving it. "It smells like heaven."

"Splash a little of that wine in the sauce. Did you see those olives? They look like goose eggs." Those gray eyes twinkled for him, the lines he'd gotten used to around Artie's mouth almost gone.

"Did you buy us mutant Christmas olives?" The words tickled him as they fell out of his mouth and he started laughing.

"Shit. If I did you can let Duke bite me. I've just never seen any that big." Artie's eyes widened as he said that line, and then they were both laughing like idiots.

He had a stitch in his side by the time it tapered off, both of them red-cheeked and gasping. "Oh. Oh, man. Merry Christmas."

"Uh-huh. You know it."

Duke leapt off the counter, hissing and spitting as Artie's cell phone went off. They shared a resigned glance as Artie answered it. "Yeah? Uh-huh. So I don't have to. Okay. Yeah. I'll be there then. Okay. Bye."

Artie whooped as he hung up. "New case, but I don't have to go in tonight. Dyler will handle the prelim. Is that a good gift or what?"

"Works for me, detective. You ready for your wine?"

"I am." The bread pan slid right in the oven and Artie set the timer before coming over to grab a glass and toast him. "To a great Christmas and a hell of a New Year, babe."

"It will be. I know it." Greg took a sip and then leaned forward, took a long, slow kiss.

Artie kissed him right back, sharing the deep red of the wine with him, warming it, making him burn.

It made his head spin, made him more than a little dizzy with the sheer power of it. "Mmm. Hey."

He got a hum in return, Artie's sticky hands grabbing his butt. "Hey."

"You're going to leave hand prints." He couldn't stop smiling. He was a fool.

"Who's gonna see?" Those lips traveled down his throat, Artie leaving little bites along his skin.

Oh.

He just hummed, shorted out as he lifted his chin. More.

He got more. Artie licked and nibbled and finally gave him a short, sharp nip right at the base, making him shiver. Those big hands squeezed his ass the whole time.

"How long does the bread have to cook?" He could get on his knees. Right here. So easy.

"Uh. I think twenty-five minutes. The timer will ding." Looking as dazed as he felt, Artie stroked his lower back, petted his upper thigh.

"Plenty of time." He worked Artie's belt open, found the zipper pull. "I want you."

"Okay. Not gonna...uhn. Argue." His hand closed around Artie while the man was trying to talk, and that sound was pure gratification, pure need.

He slid right down, lips dragging along Artie's soft T-shirt, the smell of the man just right. Just what he wanted. His tongue brushed along the strip of skin at the bottom of Artie's belly, that hot cock rubbing against his neck.

"Babe." Artie petted his cheeks before those thick fingers slid into his hair. "Oh, God, babe."

"Mmmhmm." He nuzzled in, breathed deep as his tongue slid around the base of Artie's cock, nothing but this between them right now.

Going up on tiptoe, Artie rubbed against him, the sound of Artie's deep moans addictive. Raw. Needy.

Greg turned his head, lips parted as he licked the shaft, working his way up to the tip to trace that swollen ridge. "Artie... 's good."

"Uh-huh. More. Greg. Please." He could smell how much Artie needed him, could feel it in the way the heavy balls drew up beneath.

"Yeah." Oh, God yes. Salt and heat and Artie and... Yeah. Greg closed his eyes, head bobbing nice and slow, focusing on nothing but that cock in his mouth.

Artie was trying to hurry him along, tugging at him, cussing a little, humping a lot. But none of it was gonna make him give up the feel of Artie that fast.

He had twenty-some-odd minutes and this was all his.

Greg took a deep breath, sliding his lips down to the base of Artie's cock, humming, swallowing carefully.

"Oh. Fuck. Greg..." That sounded like Artie wasn't gonna make it a minute, let alone twenty.

He pulled back, then let his lips sink back down, working it good and slow.

"Yeah. Like that. Damn." He had Artie babbling now, that deep, gruff voice rumbling for him.

One hand dropped down, started working his own cock, jacking himself in time and just aching with it. The other stroked Artie's scarred thigh, holding the man close.

Artie went nuts, pushing in, taking his mouth fast and hard. They had a hell of a circle of pleasure going, taking and giving, Artie letting him know how damned good it was.

Love. Fuck. Yes. Love, Artie. His balls went tight as he groaned, let Artie push all the way in.

Artie came for him just like that, pressing inside him, shooting into his throat. Hot. Wet. Pure Artie.

His own orgasm followed right behind, wetting his fingers, his belly, the pleasure secondary to Artie ringing inside him.

Right where Artie belonged.

"Love you, babe," Artie said, panting, petting him.

"Yeah." He grinned, kissed Artie's hip. "Love you. Damn."

They stayed that way until the timer went off, the shrill sound making them jump and laugh. "Guess I should wash my hands, huh?"

"Uh-huh. I'm going to go get clean pants. You want sweats or are we dressing for dinner?"

"Sweats are good." Artie grinned, pulling bread out of the oven. It looked like hell on a plate and smelled like heaven.

He stole a corner, popped it in his mouth, and hummed with pleasure.

"Good?" It was cute as hell how Artie still needed cooking reassurance. Stood to reason though, as the man used to order out more than he ate in. "And where did I put my wine?"

"Almost better than sex, and I don't know. I was busy." Greg laughed, wandering toward the bedroom.

Artie's laughter floated after him, the sound of Duke purring over his cream rising to twine with it.

He bent down, turned on the Christmas tree lights on his way, the colors lighting up the entire room.

There.

They were ready.

end

Touching Evil

Printed in the United States
116083LV00001B/23/A

9 781934 166031